FOOL FOR A CLIENT

ALAN LEE

SPARKLE PRESS

Fool For A Client

by Alan Lee

First Edition
Printed in USA

Cover by Sweet 'N Spicy

Formatting by Vellum

Paperback ISBN: 9798811237241

Sparkle Press

Created with Vellum

Careful readers will notice
minor liberties taken
with the legal process.
For the sake of the story,
pay no attention.
And enjoy.

Many thanks
to Brad Thompson
for his astonishing insight
into prison life.

1

Drama at the Chez August.

Normally a refined and civilized oasis, the house had grown fractious and petty to a shocking degree. Harsh words, harsher looks. Not from me, constant scholar and gentleman, but from my baser housemates, including the great love of my life turned vengeful hellcat.

A description which could, at the moment, be applied to either Ronnie or Manny.

At the root of our discontent were two sins.

The first—Manny had brought home a board game. The Settlers of Catan. As innocuous a gift as the Trojan Horse of Troy. We poured wine and learned to play and two hours later Sheriff Stackhouse stood, knocking over her chair, and she hurled the vestiges of her Pinot Gris into Timothy August's face, accused him of cheating, and she stormed out of the house, sleeping at her place. Once gone, Timothy admitted his deceit but claimed victory over his withdrawn opponent, as unfatherly an act I could ever remember him perpetrating.

Stackhouse returned the next day and apologized, and

so did Timothy. We played again. At the end of the first hour, Veronica Summers caught Stackhouse drawing more resources from the bank than she should, and declared her guilty and defended it by backward-engineering the resources Stackhouse *should* have, versus what she *did* have, reaching a verdict beyond reasonable doubt. Stackhouse countered that she'd seen Ronnie pilfer one of my Knight cards but hadn't said anything, because women should stick together, but now she could go straight to hell. The game ended prematurely with Manny and I bemoaning the fallen nature of the female. That night in bed I reproached the thievery with unconditional love and in return Ronnie planted a memory foam pillow between us and told me not to touch her.

To preserve harmony, Manny destroyed Settlers of Catan, which never should have been purchased in the first place because Catan wasn't even in America, he said, and instead replaced it with Agricola, a board game solidly set in America's noble Midwest.

We played the first game to its conclusion, more or less civil, each player too new to the rules to break them.

Near the end of our second game, I advanced my farmhouse from clay to stone, thereby blocking Manny from doing the same, virtually ensuring my victory, and he accused me of poor sportsmanship. I accused him of being a nincompoop and he threw—*threw*—the board across the room and he walked upstairs. The pieces showered onto Georgina Princess August, faithful hound, who looked worried her home was being destroyed from within with internecine childishness.

Tonight, Manny was arranging the board again. A third game. The atmosphere was charged, for all parties had behaved poorly and expressed regret but couldn't promise they would represent themselves better tonight, their passions beyond control.

Except for Mackenzie August, a saint and as steady as the Rock of Gibraltar.

The tension was somewhat relieved by my son, Kix, who had helped himself to a glass of margarita. Manny had set the glass down to arrange the board, and Kix wandered over and availed himself to as much as he could —less than a third of the glass—before Manny made a gasp and snatched it away.

Now Kix was trying and failing to climb onto the couch, laughing hysterically with each failure, while Ronnie and Stackhouse cried with mirth over this development, monsters both of them, and I was researching what to do with a drunken child—experts agreed he would survive a small accidental ingestion of tequila, and there would be no brain damage, and it might even help him relax around cute girls.

This, however, was only half.

The second root of our discontent—my father had hired a housekeeper. Once a week the villain would clean the house, top to bottom. Today had been her second effort.

Neither Manny nor I could imagine a worse betrayal. And from my own father.

It's not for your mess, Timothy had explained last week. It's for mine.

No it's not, said Stackhouse. It's for mine. That chivalry would gall me if I had one ounce less self-awareness, but half of everything I own ends up on this poor man's bedroom floor. We need help.

The housekeeper is for me too, confessed Ronnie, who, despite being one of the most driven and competent women I knew, could not wash a pot or iron a skirt without liberal use of profanity.

Perhaps, Manny politely explained, you three immature adolescent Russian panhandlers could grow up and take care of yourselves. You think George Washington had a housekeeper?

Yes, said Timothy August, I suspect he did.

Bien, said Manny. Defeat the British single-handedly and I'll be quiet, *señor.*

One should not outsource the work of being human, I explained. Caring for ourselves and for our home and loved ones is the reason we're alive. It's good for you. Done correctly, the joy it brings—

At that point, I was advised to shove my sermonizing up my ass.

Now, Manny was setting up the Agricola board and searching the rules for any possible advantage, and he was complaining that the table was streaky because the housekeeper used inferior cleaners, and Ronnie was reading emails beside me, running her fingers on the back of my neck, and she was smiling at Kix, and I put down my phone, satisfied Kix would live, and I pressed my thumb along the arm of the couch.

"She's not conditioning the leather," I said.

"Mackenzie," said my wife. My blonde athletic wife who smelled of perfume.

"She's not. The leather is shiny and it sticks to my thumb."

"No it doesn't," she said.

"It does on a molecular level. We should fire Helga."

"Her name is Helena. And we don't pay her to condition the couch."

"I cannot imagine a better use of her time," I said.

"You should see our bathroom, babe." Stackhouse swirled her goblet of red. She had changed out of her Sheriff garb and she wore pajamas—silken pants and a top that plunged so deeply that even Ronnie was admiring the view. "The floor is visible. It's a miracle."

"I'd forgotten what color the tiles were," said Timothy, beside her on the love seat, opposite me and Ronnie.

But seriously, said Kix. *You have GOT to try that lemonade. I'm being totally serious, guys.*

"The point is," said Stackhouse, with a fond look at Kix on the ground, "Helena is a miracle worker, and she has better things to do than massage your couch."

"Besides. You and Manny are *good* at massaging your own couch," said Ronnie.

"Sarcasm is the language of the weak," I said.

"But don't you and Manny prefer to handle it yourself?" Ronnie's eyes twinkled. They sparkled. They shimmered.

"George Washington didn't use sarcasm," said Manny, at the table. "Nor did he make dirty jokes. This is why I don't let Beck play."

"Did she ask?" Ronnie wore pajamas too but hers had a high crew neck. Which was, I thought, a ludicrous way to spend two hundred dollars.

"To play board games? Of course she asked."

"You said *no*?"

"You two *pechugonas* are bad influences," he said.

"What's a—"

"Don't ask. It's flattering. Kinda," I said.

"You have to let Beck play," said Ronnie.

"She would lose her faith in humanity. Your behavior is floorable."

"Deplorable."

When did this couch get so tall, said Kix. *And unstable? I am mortified.*

"Tell me again." Stackhouse drank deeply from her red. "Why are we playing this? I might shoot someone."

"To prove we can, *señorita*. Otherwise we're no better than bittering countries in the Middle East. And so I can win."

"Bickering."

"Mackenzie, shut up," he said. "I said what I said. It's a new word you don't know about. The game's ready."

Ronnie stood and stretched, like a cat, like my favorite cat. "I'll be on my best behavior. I'm hoping to get lucky later, and the man I love has high standards."

"Obey the ten commandments, is my only request. If sex is on the table, I'll reduce it to the top six."

"Sex better not be on the table." Manny looked at the board with a critical eye.

"Not recently." Ronnie smiled at the world and the memories.

But what IS sex? Kix was lying on his back, losing steam. *I've heard it discussed in the highest terms. Also bring me a bottle of that lemonade, please. You would not believe the hit of serotonin it provides, but now I'm feeling sluggish.*

"Kix said sex," said Stackhouse and she laughed about it.

"Proud moment for a grandfather," said Timothy and he did not laugh.

"I'll put him to bed quick, so he won't witness Manny's meltdown." I picked my son up and he said, *Whoa, go slow.*

A knock at the door.

It was late.

Timothy answered it and said, "Ah. This must be for you, darling Sheriff."

I walked up the stairs and caught a glimpse of two plainclothes Roanoke City detectives in the doorway trying not to look down Stackhouse's pajamas.

I brushed Kix's teeth with an Elmo toothbrush and an Orajel toothpaste, something he liked to attempt on his own on nights he didn't pound margaritas. I kissed his head and apologized for my lack of vigilance, but he fell asleep before reaching the crib. I said a prayer that his heavenly father would cover the insufficiencies of his earthly father, and I tucked him in.

I returned downstairs, prepared for war.

The detectives in the doorway watched me. Ronnie and Timothy watched me. Stackhouse looked irritated. I felt like Scarlett O'Hara descending a grand staircase with the attention.

"This is about the margarita," I said.

"Hey, August, sorry for the late intrusion," said Detective Green.

I knew them both by sight.

I'd worked with the White guy, Detective Green, former detective in Roanoke County, now in the city. Trim, good-looking, sharp cheekbones, wore lot of gel in his hair, and I thought his shoulders looked too bunched up. He wore stylish jeans and a windbreaker.

The other guy, Detective Archie Hart, was shorter and rounder, Black, and I thought he looked like James Bond's friend Felix. Archie wore an actual overcoat, like a detective in the fifties.

"Mackenzie," said Stackhouse. "Babe, these two jackasses want to ask you questions, but they won't tell me why, and I might pepper-spray them."

"Can they ask while I dominate at Agricola?"

"No we can't. But we'd come in, if we're invited, otherwise we gotta do it tomorrow."

Stackhouse stood in the doorway, arms crossed, a physical barrier, but I told them to come in. They did, edging around the sheriff like she'd scald them. She wasn't their boss; they were police, she was sheriff's department, separate entities. But still, one doesn't anger the sheriff, any sheriff, especially not Stackhouse.

Archie Hart was trying not to ogle her and Ronnie. He ducked his head to both and said, "Ma'am."

"Don't ma'am me," said Stackhouse.

"Sorry about the mess," said Manny. "Woman named Olga got everything dirty."

"Are you kidding. This might be the cleanest place I've been," said Archie.

"It's like a cow was slaughtered in here, *amigo*."

"August, we have questions about a homicide. Two separate homicides, actually," said Green.

"Sounds fun. But I haven't worked a homicide recently."

"This isn't about homicides you worked. You want to talk alone?"

"Like hell he does," said Ronnie. "I'm his attorney and I'll be present."

"Which homicide?" said Stackhouse.

"I'm advising Mackenzie to keep silent," said Ronnie.

"You guys want a drink?" I said.

Archie considered but said, "No thanks."

"Talk all you want, Mackenzie isn't saying a word." Ronnie, a defense attorney, was a firm believer that you didn't tell the cops a thing.

"I was told you'd be here, Ms. Summers," said Detective Green. "Excuse me, is it Mrs. August?"

"At the moment it's Counselor Summers."

"All we want to do is check Mack off our list. And I brought you something." He carried an iPad in a leather binder. He opened the binder, twitched out a paper, and offered it to Ronnie, who didn't touch it yet. "A signed statement of confidentiality."

"Confidentiality? Why?" said Stackhouse.

"So August and his attorney can answer questions without worry we'll use it against them."

The hairs on the back of my neck raised.

Ronnie took the letter and read it.

"Signed by who?" said Stackhouse.

"Me and the Commonwealth's Attorney," said Detective Green.

"Tom signed this?" Stackhouse set down the wine. "What the hell is going on?"

"I don't get it," said Timothy. "Explain it to a layman outside law enforcement."

"The detectives want to ask me questions about two homicides," I said. "But anything I say can and will be used against me. Ergo, I won't answer. To allay my fear, they have a statement promising nothing said tonight will ever be used as evidence in a court of law, and they took the extra step of going to the highest prosecutor in Roanoke City and getting his signature."

Ronnie handed the letter to Stackhouse.

"That doesn't mean Mackenzie will respond to questions," said Ronnie.

Green held out his hands, as though appealing to a jury. "Look. Archie and me, we don't want to be here. We want to be home watching Netflix. Okay? This sucks. We came at night as a courtesy—fewer prying eyeballs. We respect each other here, or I hope, and we can do this quick and professional."

"Sit," I said. "Ask."

"You want to talk alone?"

"Not without me," said Stackhouse, "and if you two little shits have a problem with that I'll wake up the Chief of Police and demand you work parking meters until you quit. Ask your questions."

"I'm listening too." Manny might've carried the most weight with the detectives. He was a local legend. He was leaning against the couch, sleeves rolled up, his arms crossed and muscular, tattoos showing. He'd taken to wearing a leather bracelet made by his nephew in Puerto Rico. His shoulders were broad, his waist narrow, his brow was furrowed, and the detectives acted aware of him the way rookie ballplayers would be aware of an angry Michael Jordan. "And if you two little shits have a problem with that, I'm going *azotar tu trasero hasta que sangres.*"

Archie said, "Mr. August, you don't remember but I helped with the Sanders fiasco when—"

"Talk faster," said Stackhouse.

Archie flinched and nodded.

Both detectives sat at the dining table.

"Mr. August, did you know Don Torres?"

"Mackenzie has no comment," said Ronnie.

"This is off the record. Nothing he says—"

"He has no comment."

Green took a deep breath. Steeled himself.

"How about this. Let's us do some give and take. I'm the lead investigator in two homicides, which means I don't ever divulge my investigative findings. But I'll bend a little, out of respect for you, August. Don Torres was murdered and I have evidence you were there when he died."

Timothy August made a noise like sucking too much air. The rest of us were still. In the course of events in our shared history, there had been some violence. We didn't know where this fit yet.

"I was there when Don Torres died," I repeated. "That's a question, not a statement."

"Evidence suggests it."

"Name doesn't ring a bell. Show me a photograph," I said and Ronnie didn't object.

"Sure."

"Detective," said Stackhouse. "You're implying Mackenzie is a suspect in the homicide?"

"It's more like," said Archie, "we want to verify Mackenzie *isn't* a suspect."

"Don't patronize us with clunky rhetoric, Detective. It's late and you're sitting in our dining room," Ronnie snapped.

"Okay." Green made hard eye contact with me, and he held up his hands, like—*I got nothing to hide.* "Mack's a suspect in both homicides."

"Both," I said.

"Correct."

"How many suspects do you have?" asked Ronnie.

"Just one, Counselor Summers."

"This," I said, "is far more interesting than Agricola."

2

Green set his iPad on the table. On screen was a photograph of a man I didn't know. The guy had a big face, bushy hair and eyebrows, swarthy skin.

"Donald Torres," said Mr. Green.

"Torres. I remember this," said Stackhouse. "Found two weeks ago."

None of us had killed anyone in the last two weeks. So that was nice.

"I don't know him," I said.

"One minute, Detective. I will brief my client for sixty seconds." Ronnie grabbed my arm and she walked me through the kitchen and onto the back deck and she closed the door.

It was 8:30pm, early spring. It was dark and misty and chilly.

"Mackenzie, you need to proceed with caution."

"You think I killed Don Torres."

"Don't be an ass, I know you didn't. A handsome ass, I should clarify. Even though you're innocent, and even though they brought a signed statement of confidentiality, those detectives aren't your allies. Detectives are supposed to follow the facts, but sometimes they're just bastards. Don't say anything. And if you do, and I pinch you, close your mouth," she said.

I had a rolodex of jokes about how she forgot what I did for a living. But she was not in a jocular mood and I respected her.

"Yes ma'am," I said.

"You didn't kill Don Torres. But did you know him?"

"No," I said.

"How confident are you? Because they have leverage they haven't revealed yet."

"I don't recognize the name or face. And I would."

"You've been busy with cases recently," she said.

"I would remember."

"Okay. Don't tell them anything. I pinch, you hush." She opened the door and walked me back, and I felt the glow of being lovingly manhandled.

I sat. She stood behind me.

"Detectives, proceed," she said.

Green nodded. "You don't know Don Torres."

"No," I said.

"You were in his house."

"Location?" I said.

"A brick ranch in north Roanoke City, near Williamson. 12 Forrest Hill Avenue."

I searched the recent past.

"Two weeks ago?" I said.

"You tell me."

"Try again," said Ronnie.

Green pursed his lips. "Ten days ago."

"I haven't been in that part of town in the previous two weeks," I said.

"We have DNA that suggests other wise."

Mackenzie August, a little stunned.

"What form of DNA evidence?" said Ronnie.

Green swiped on the iPad screen and a new face appeared. Good hair, big smile, like posing for a headshot.

"Jason Hicks. Did you know him?"

"Looks familiar," I said, and Ronnie pinched me.

"He's a local realtor. His face is everywhere," said Green. "*Was* a local realtor."

"That's how I know him. Never met him though."

"Did you go to his house?"

"Is my DNA there too?" I said.

Ronnie pinched me and I hated it.

"Have you been to the home of Jason Hicks?" said Green.

"No."

"He lives a mile from here, in the Wasena area. *Lived* a mile from here."

"In the last two weeks, I haven't been inside any home in the Wasena neighborhood," I said.

Green and Archie looked at one another.

"Mr. August, can you account for your whereabouts on Thursday?" Archie produced a stylus for his own iPad.

"Thursday last week?"

"Yes sir, " said Archie.

"I dropped Kix off at school and left for West Virginia. I returned around one in the morning," I said.

"What were you doing in West Virginia?"

"Working a case."

"What kinda case?"

"If that becomes germane," I said, "I'll tell you."

"It's important," said Green.

"Not enough."

"August—"

"I didn't do the thing you're suggesting. I didn't kill these men. I have no fear of the truth, and my innocence will soon be shining in your eyeballs like the golden sun. At the moment, I see no reason to void the promised confidentiality of my client. And I'm only not mocking you because my lawyer is mean."

"How about this, Mr. August. Can anyone not related to the case vouch that you were in West Virginia?" said Archie.

That was tricky. I'd been out of state chasing a runaway wife, and I hadn't found her. I'd found nothing, in fact, a complete whiff.

"I got drive-thru Chick-fil-A," I said, and it was lame.

"Paid with a card?"

"Cash."

"We can pull your phone's data." Archie was making notes on his own iPad. Technology! "If you made phone calls or texts, we'll see they came from West Virginia?"

"That's right," I said, but we knew the truth—I could've swung by a house and killed someone on my way out of town. It didn't take long.

"What about April 3rd?" said Green.

I drew the phone from my pocket and opened my calendar. I scrolled.

"A Tuesday. All over town. Home late that evening," I said.

"Working with anyone?"

"Working alone. Insurance fraud, taking photos."

I had no alibis. For either day.

How about that.

"How were they murdered?" I said.

"You tell us."

"I swear to God," said Stackhouse.

"Ay, Sheriff, when did Roanoke City start hiring little *pendejos*?" said Manny.

Stackhouse stood from the arm of the couch. "I'm getting my mace."

Green held ups his hands. He was sweating and it showed along his hairline. "Okay, *okay*."

"Mr. August, because this was in the news, I'll tell you something," said Archie. He was leaning away from Green, in case things were thrown. "They were beaten to death. Blunt force trauma to the head."

"What evidence suggests I was there?" I said.

"Listen." Green flipped closed the leather binder. "We know you didn't do it. Or we assume so. We have a lot of respect for you and what you do. But that's all I'm sharing. We came hoping you had airtight alibis, that you were in Florida, that you were in Africa, that you were on the moon, but you don't. No big deal, only means you're on my list a few more days before we catch the right guy." He jerked his chin at Archie. "Let's leave these nice people alone."

"August," said Archie. He made eye contact with me two seconds too long. "I'll see you soon. Okay?"

I nodded and saw them out, the detectives' footsteps too loud and too slow, no one else moving, the whole thing awkward. Each man got into his own car and drove away, headlights punching cones through the damp air.

I remained on the front porch long enough for Archie to circle the block and return. He parked, brakes squeaking, and he opened the driver door, motor still running. Hurried up my sidewalk and he spoke soft.

"I'm not here."

"You're not here," I said. "You went home to watch Netflix."

"This one's deep off the record, Mr. August. Deep deep."

"I understand," I said.

"Detective Green, you know, he's good at the work. Takes it seriously, but maybe he can be an asshole about it. I'll tell you what we got, as a favor, because you've always been good to the force."

"I appreciate it."

"I don't know if this'll help you and, again, you didn't hear it from me. At each crime scene, there was a struggle. Both Torres and Hicks put up a fight, both died from head wounds. Most likely killed with the same hammer, looks like, though we don't have the hammer."

I nodded. "Okay."

"Your DNA was found under the fingernails of both men. Skin cells. Like the person they'd been fighting was you. I know that's bad news, but there it is. Without the alibis, I know Green's already decided your ass is cooked. Sorry, August."

Archie turned and ran back to the idling car.

Jiminy Christmas. The victims had my skin under their nails?

Maybe I'd killed them and forgotten.

3

"One of the reasons the detectives came last night," said Ronnie, "was to examine your arms and your hands, and maybe your face and neck. If the victims had your skin under their nails, you were clawed."

"I am blemish free, fortunately," I said.

"It has to be a forensic error."

She and I stood in the kitchen drinking coffee. Kix babbled from his high chair.

I'd slept great, secure in my innocence. Ronnie slept fitfully, juggling rage and panic. Maybe doubt too, though she didn't admit it, and who could blame her.

She said, "The DNA samples were mismatched. Or they have incompetent lab technicians. Or they have the wrong Mackenzie. Or *something.*"

"It's possible."

But it wasn't likely, and we both knew it.

"Or you were framed."

"Also possible," I said.

Also unlikely. But more probable of the two options.

"You're too calm about this, Mackenzie."

"I am not too calm. The day is too early."

I don't feel great, said Kix. *Like I'm thirsty but there's not enough water in the world.*

"They have your DNA on file from old cases?" she said.

"Yes. Multiple."

"I'll gather hair samples and scrape your arm for skin, and I'll arrange for another test from a private lab, whose techs aren't mouth-breathers," said Ronnie.

"There should be hair in the bathroom. Helga is terrible at her job," I said. "Or, even better, maybe she framed me."

"Helena," said Ronnie. "Her name is Helena, and she's frail and cancerous and she didn't frame you."

"Cancerous?"

"She had a double mastectomy in February, but the cancer had already spread and now she's in radiation. She's a tiny woman with no hair."

Perhaps, I thought, Helga could be forgiven for not conditioning the leather.

Ronnie said, "Your father hired her because she's broke."

"Doesn't mean she didn't pilfer my DNA from the drain."

"Your DNA was scraped from under the fingernails of both men before Helena started. It couldn't be her."

I nodded.

A shame. I'd like it if Helga was in prison.

"You didn't think of that?" she said.

Ronnie wore high heels. Not the flirty kind, but the kind an irate and domineering CEO would wear on a day she needed heads to roll. With it she wore a modish blazer with the sleeves rolled, and the flaring white shirt cuffs were visible. She wore a black pencil skirt too, made by Spanx, but I wasn't allowed to tell anyone because they'd get the wrong idea.

I loved skirts and I loved Spring.

Skirts were absent before the Spring
But proud-pied April, dressed in all his trim,
Put the spirit of youth into everything.

...

Certainly I was botching that.

"Mackenzie?" said Ronnie. "Please focus. You're being too cavalier. Based on the order of events, you should have realized Helena couldn't possibly frame you."

I raised my coffee.

"The fault lies with the sun. And I prefer to force facts to fit my theory," I said.

"Not even I could convince a jury that a small woman in radiation could overpower two grown men."

"Wait until they discover our table is streaky."

Ronnie smiled. Some of the tension drained from her shoulders.

"Husband. Why are you jealous of poor Helena?"

"Imagine you discovered that I hired a woman to scratch my back."

"Scratching your back is my job," said Ronnie.

"Precisely."

"This is materially different."

"You hired a woman to do my job," I said.

"No, your father hired a woman to do *my* job. And his. And Stackhouse's."

"I take care of my own house."

"She reduces my stress," said Ronnie.

"She does not."

"She does! Mackenzie, I feel guilty not running the

laundry or scrubbing the shower. You don't imply that I should, but I do anyway. Now there's no guilt, because even though I'm not physically handling it, I'm financially handling it."

"*You* are?"

"Um," she said.

"You pay Helga? I thought Timothy did."

"Does it matter?"

"There are degrees to infidelity," I said.

She set down her coffee. Rubbed her eyes and crossed her arms. "I charge my clients three hundred dollars an hour. I can afford Helena once a week."

"It's not about the revenue/expense report."

"Mackenzie, your father found her, and I offered to—"

"Judas!" I said. "Benedict Arnold! Fredo!"

"Who is Fredo?"

"Michael Corleone's brother in *The Godfather*, who betrayed and tried to murder his family. This is worse," I said.

"Hiring a housekeeper is not worse than killing your brother! And getting angry with me gets you nowhere, Mackenzie, because I think it's hot."

"Do you."

"Strangely so. You grow taller and broader."

Sex, said Kix. *Is this about sex? It sounds like it's about sex.*

"Wow."

"If Kix doesn't watch his language, we'll be getting a call from his school," said Ronnie. She played with Kix's hair.

I knew it. This is about sex. Are we out of that fancy lemonade from last night? Because I could go for a roadie.

I DROVE KIX TO SCHOOL, pleading with him to use other words, like dog or cat or defenestrate or probable cause or fastball or Juan Soto. He made no promises. Roanoke's finest Montessori school thought the world of Kix but held me and my Honda Accord in lower regard, and the nice staff accepted him each morning pleasantly surprised that he'd survived the night. If he started spouting off about sex...

I opted against mentioning the margarita.

My office was on Campbell Avenue, over a restaurant that changed ownership frequently. It was now a taco place. Recently every place was a taco place. I was hoping for French cuisine next—Blue Apron and Red Rooster had gone out of business.

The hundred-year-old wooden stairs welcomed me with groans, and I left the office door open to vent the radiated heat. My desk sat opposite the doorway, so I could see whoever came in, I could duck if they carried Patriot missiles. To the right of the doorway were three tall windows and a set of bookshelves. The bookshelves were ornamental but they did support my bowl of potpourri, recently refreshed with a gentleman's blend.

Georgina Princess had taken to lying in the hallway, exceedingly offended by the new blend. That and she wanted to keep an eye on the travel agent down the hall, a man far too kind not to be a serial killer. The guy wrote a travel blog. I'd sampled a few posts. He was a serial killer and an abuser of split infinitives. I cannot, *cannot*, abide more than one per page, much less one per paragraph.

Today I'd left GPA at home, providing an olfactory sabbatical.

I sat and considered my professional domain.

Multiple cases lay open within it. A recent surge of

business had followed articles written about me in *People* magazine, and then in the local newspaper. I was dubbed The Great American Sleuth, and I was rejecting more clients than ever. Ronnie said I was famous, but the whole affair ruffled my feathers. Not like I was a proud peacock, but rather a pissed-off bird.

My current cases were—

-I was trying and failing to find a runaway wife. She was way gone into the Midwest, and my client was out of money. Privately I determined she was better off without him. As of today, I'd be done. Case closed but not solved. I needed to debrief him and move on.

-I was gathering evidence in an insurance fraud case for State Farm. My client had expressed amazement and gratitude at my results and asked for more.

-Brad Thompson had hired me to investigate a violent crime in Salem. His client claimed innocence but they needed proof. I'd provided some, based on testimony and forensic anomalies, and now I was on stand-by.

-Next week I was scheduled to serve subpoenas on five extremely hard-to-locate persons. I didn't enjoy process serving, but I'd been paid an extremely hard-to-decline retainer. Enough to afford more sets of Ronnie's pajamas.

I propped my feet on the wooden desk and leaned back in the swivel chair and opened the drawer so I could see the bottle of Johnny Walker Blue, and drew fortitude from the sight. I called my client and told him his wife was in Kansas now, if she hadn't moved on, and tracking her further would require too much manpower and money. I would send him an email with my findings. He raged and I listened, and I suggested that he go to an AA meeting before trying Tinder Mingle or whatever singles used to find love. He told me I was a *** and I could *** and he hung up.

Next I called Dean Law and explained that personal matters threatened next week. I couldn't promise the subpoenas would be served in seven-to-ten days, and I was willing to refund the retainer. The nice office manager said to do my best and say hello to Ronnie Summers for her.

I stood. I cracked my knuckles. I stretched my neck. I twisted side to side, like I thought a sprinter would do before his Olympic event.

I had a new client.

It was me.

I was, I thought, one of my better looking clients. And one of the more innocent.

Now to prove it.

I left downtown in my Honda Accord, which still felt new, like a spaceship, and drove north on Williamson to 12 Forrest Hill Avenue.

Home of Donald Torres, deceased.

The neighborhood was hard-working blue collar, not indigent blue collar. These homeowners had pride. The house was as Green claimed, a brick ranch. The driveway needed to be resealed with blacktop. The lawn had clearly been fertilized and weeded last year, though now with spring's arrival it required a mowing. No fence. No swing-set in the back. No evidence of a dog. The minimal amount of shrubs. Don's home showed less care than his neighbors, but not an absence of it.

I watched the house. I willed myself to remember being here.

But it wouldn't work. I never had been.

I made a note on my phone—*where was his car?*

I brought up his photo and I glared at it too. Ineffective. I'd never met this man.

Ronnie rang. It startled me like I'd been doing something wrong.

"I'm not doing anything wrong."

She said, "I finished storming the courthouse, and I yelled at anything that moved. Those cowards couldn't look at me. They're taking this seriously, Mackenzie. As though you *actually* beat two men to death with a hammer. The Commonwealth's Attorney, Tom Holloway? He's recusing himself. So is Judge Thomas. I know where both men live, and I might drive by their houses and tell their wives they married pansies."

"Drink a cup of coffee first. Then decide."

"Are you impressed I said pansy? Not the better word?" said Ronnie.

"You are Mother Teresa."

"What are you doing?"

"Snooping around the Torres estate."

"I am your attorney, and this is my counsel—please don't make my job more difficult."

"No promises," I said. "Should we hire a different attorney so there's no conflict of interest?"

"Yes. If you want me to cut that attorney's throat."

"Ah."

"Don't get caught."

I snorted. "Caught."

4

I stood out of the car and donned latex gloves.

The crime scene had been released. Despite being a suspect, I wasn't trespassing on the property, not unless Don's estate filed a restraining order against me.

In the back, I walked down the bunker stairs to the basement door. Leaves had clotted the drain. There was no deadbolt, and I forced the lock and walked in. *Now* I was trespassing.

You always knew when you'd entered an empty house. The vacancy was held in the seams.

Torres' basement was unfinished. The floor was flecked concrete, the walls exposed cinderblock, the ceiling exposed rafters and plumbing and power and duct work.

Directly across from me sat a Maytag washer and dryer, which looked newly purchased.

The wall to my right was floor-to-ceiling shelves built with 2x4s and plywood. Each shelf held a blue plastic storage bin, labeled by permanent marker with words like SUMMER and XMAS and MUSIC and BLANKETS and

BOOKS. The lids were loosely set on the bins, a sign of police investigation.

The basement was otherwise empty. I admired the fastidiousness, but something about it bugged me. I turned in a circle twice and took photos with my phone. Wearing gloves, I tilted the bins to look inside each and they appeared to be accurately labeled. The nagging sensation remained but I couldn't place it.

I took the exposed wooden staircase to the main level, arriving in the narrow hallway. To the left was the living room and kitchen. To the right, bedrooms.

Donald Torres had died next to his mattress. A stain of brown marked where his head lay, clumps of hair still matted into it. Technicians had scrapped several gouges through the stain, taking the best samples of blood and hair.

The struggle must have been brief. The nightstand was still upright. The bed showed signs of police inspection but not a violent struggle. The window blinds were intact. A hammer had been used, Archie said, but I saw no holes in the wall, no chunks missing from the dresser, from wayward blows. I clicked on the phone's flashlight and inspected the ceiling fan—dark spatter on one of the blades. Evidence of blunt force trauma to the skull, but not a messy slaughter, more like one big thunk.

White powder was snowed on the doorknob and every flat surface. Strips of tape had removed fingerprints—several clean rectangles in the powder on the nightstand.

The room was spartan. No television. No pictures, no paintings. The comforter looked like a Target brand, and the furniture was cheap, the kind that arrived in the mail to be assembled. Neat sock drawer. Three pairs of pants in the closet and five white shirts. One sports coat, no suits. I guessed he worked a white collar job, but not in management. Like a human resources assistant or something professional without the responsibility. Otherwise he'd have to dress better.

He shaved with Gillette and washed with Head & Shoulders. The drains in the sink and shower had been taken for evidence.

Access to the police report would be nice, but that would be issued to an attorney after charges were made. Or after Ronnie threatened to kill enough people. I didn't know what had been taken as evidence. For example, Don Torres's phone. His bills. His laptop, his wallet.

The spare bedroom was empty but for an exercise rowing machine on the floor.

A large rug in the television room had been vacuumed, probably by the forensic team when they realized they had no suspects. Other than me. The space was decorated with a matching couch and La-Z-Boy chair, faux brown leather. Two pillows and one throw—looked like Don enjoyed couch naps in front of a good show. Television on a wooden stand in the corner, with an attached Roku box. Coffee table with two remotes.

Don smoked cigarettes here. The yellow scent of ash was still in the walls and fabric, even weeks after his final drag, and there was an ashtray stand between the chair and couch.

The kitchen was like a showroom in its simplicity. Torres had clearly been a bachelor living a simple life. A few plates, a few coffee mugs, minimal cutlery. His mail was opened on the little table in the corner. One bill from Roanoke Gas, one from the Water Authority, one from Cox Cable. I opened drawers and found older mail, including a cell phone bill, which I pocketed, but no credit card bills, no credit card offers, no mortgage statements.

That was odd. Why was that odd?

I'd been looking at Donald wrong.

He hadn't been living simply. He hadn't been living here at all, until the last few months. He was new to the house. That's why he had so few belongings.

Did he own it? On my phone I opened Roanoke County's parcel viewer and searched the address—yes, owned by Donald Torres. No middle name.

I called the Water Authority and used his information from the bill to pretend I was Torres and I learned he'd activated service in November, and he hadn't transferred the service over from another local house. The nice lady thought it was an odd question.

So Torres was either new to the area or he'd been renting from a place that supplied water.

What else was I missing?

I made a note on my phone—*where were his pay stubs? Where did he work?*

He didn't work from home. I'd found no office, or even a computer.

I paced the house again, wondering what I overlooked.

"I can't imagine," I said, "why I killed such a boring guy."

I left through the same door I entered, followed by the nagging sensation.

Pay attention, Mackenzie, the sensation whispered. You missed it.

5

The home of Jason Hicks was a different story. His family was there with a U-Haul moving truck.

He lived in Wasena, within walking distance of the Tap Room and the Greenway. His home was a two-story brick colonial. The bricks were bright with sunlight. The shutters were black and plastic, and the trim was white, and the lawn had sharp edges, mulched with brown shredded wood, and his hyacinths and tulips were in full bloom. An American flag flapped on the angled post jutting beside the front door. The curb appeal was strong, like its owner knew he would be judged.

I parked a block away and watched, and I pulled Jason Hicks up on Facebook.

He appeared to be single. Good-looking, the boy next door. Clean shaven, hair combed to the side. The owner of a handsome brown Lab. I scrolled. Jason was a realtor. Former student at Cave Spring High School and Roanoke College. Had a girlfriend...last year, looked like. Went out with friends a lot.

I'd assumed the folks walking into and out of his house were his family. But if he was single…?

I removed a pair of Nikon binoculars from the dashboard, the kind with a camera. I could record anything I saw, and I'd used them enough it would be fair to call me creepy. I zoomed in on the house and the persons there.

This was Jason's extended family; they looked like him. That was his father and his brother, I'd bet my car on it. The same smooth all-American faces. They were carrying bags to the moving truck. Jason had been dead for seven days, and his family was moving through the grieving process. Cleaning out the house, claiming certain items of importance to remember Jason, maybe arguing over expensive televisions or blenders or whatever.

I'd never been to this house.

I wasn't positive I'd even been on this street, Howbert, near 11th.

Had Jason been killed in his bedroom? I couldn't ask his mom; I had scruples. Was he dating anyone? What was on his phone?

Why the heck had my DNA been under Jason Hicks' fingernails?

I watched the family, large in my lenses, until I felt intrusive and I looked through Jason's photos on Facebook and Instagram. He might have other social media accounts, like Tick Tock or Chat Snapped or whatever, but those places were far too trendy to let me in.

Did Manny have those? He could be kinda girly. I texted him.

-Do you have Tick Tock?

>> Like a watch?

-No

>> I wear RGM, made in USA, because EFF Putin

-Not a watch. It's a social media thing

>> You think RGM is too old fashioned? I might get a Autodromo.

-Not a watch, you goon. What about Chat Snapped?

-Wait. No. I googled it. It's called Snap Chat.

>> What about it? This is boring.

-Do you have an account?

>> No

>> I bet Putin uses snap chat

>> I got to go. I am important.

>> Don't kill anyone with a hammer.

Manny Martinez, not always helpful.

Jason Hicks and Don Torres were as different as could be.

Jason was young and handsome.

Don was late middle-aged and bushy.

Jason's home was lovingly tended.

Don barely touched his.

Jason was active online.

I found no trace of Don Torres anywhere, including Linked-In.

Jason was proud of his job.

Don's was obscure.

What did they have in common? Male, lived in Roanoke, killed with a hammer, had my DNA under their nails.

And they both knew I wasn't their killer.

6

The secret to fried rice is that the rice can't be fresh. The grains need to be cooked but then refrigerated overnight, so they can dry, otherwise the rice will be mushy and why bother.

Preparing for dinner the night before was beyond the reach of most men. But not for Mackenzie August. He'd cooked and refrigerated rice last night, even in the face of the electric chair. I was unconcerned; there wasn't enough electricity in the world.

Ronnie had purchased a gas griddle for the back deck. A four-burner Pit Boss—a name I'd suggested would work for me in the bedroom, but didn't land when she tried it. I turned on the burners and five minutes later the surface was hot enough and I poured a healthy amount of olive oil onto the griddle and spread my chopped chicken thighs on one side, and the rice onto the other. I added onions to the chicken and then garlic and carrots, folding the mixture over and over with the long flat spatula, and over the chicken I sprinkled salt and pepper and ginger. I flipped the rice and added pats of butter and soy sauce.

The denouement approached and I combined the rice and chicken into a satisfying mountain, and I cracked two eggs into the mountain and let it fry one more minute before scooping the banquet into a bowl.

I entered the house with a sizzling, savory, non-mushy feast.

I set the bowl onto the middle of the table with a big spoon, so the family could help itself. I spooned some onto Kix's tray and he sighed and said, *Imma make a mess and you're going to be frustrated, but there's no tidy way for me to eat this, and I've told you but you didn't listen.*

Manny wasn't home yet. Stackhouse took the far end of the table with her wine. Ronnie sat beside Kix and began picking the chicken and carrots out from the rice, in mortal terror of excess carbohydrates. Timothy lowered across from me with a heaping plate.

"So?" he said. "Did you kill them?"

"That's not funny," said Stackhouse.

"Oh, come on."

"It's not."

"You know what I meant. It's hard on a father, worrying the whole day, and I wanted to lighten the mood. Mackenzie and Manny crack jokes all the time," said Timothy.

"They're allowed to."

"I'm not?"

"Morbid humor is earned at crime scenes." Stackhouse hadn't dressed in sheriff garb today, but a skirt and blouse. She wore a pearl necklace and she was absently twisting one of the pearls. She didn't look hungry; she looked tired. "I don't come here for your jokes, Mr. August. I come here to be in the presence of a wise, handsome, self-possessed man in total control of himself. Not a nervous joke-teller. I deal with jackass jokers ten hours a day. What I need from you is sexy stability. At this house, I play the fool, you play the straight man, and it keeps me sane, and in return I satisfy your wishes several nights a week."

"Yuck," I said.

Ronnie smiled. "That was darling."

Sex, said Kix. *Right? It's always about sex?*

"Ask your question again, Timothy." Stackhouse steadied her eyes on him and grinned. Though subtle, it was the shift from work to woman. "But ask it like you're Paul Newman."

"I have too much dignity."

"Please. For me."

Timothy cleared his throat and set his fork down. "Son, enlighten us how—"

"If you ask it like you're Paul Newman, I'm leaving," I said.

"For Christ sake." Timothy smacked his hand on the table. "My boy is a murder suspect and no one will tell me what the hell happened today. Somebody talk or you'll all be sleeping somewhere else tonight, everyone but my grandson."

"Well done, Mr. August," said Stackhouse and she drank.

"I'm almost positive," I said, "that I didn't kill those men. I visited their homes, I looked at their photos, nothing rings a bell." I scooped more chicken and rice onto Kix's plate.

"You were framed."

"Possibly," I said.

"Or the police fumbled it," said Ronnie.

"It happens," said Stackhouse. "Too often."

"For the sake of Archie, our source, I didn't push the issue today. But tomorrow I'll attempt to subpoena the evidence, or find some way to make myself a headache with the Freedom of Information Act."

"Attempt to?" said Timothy.

"This is complicated. Mackenzie hasn't been charged. The case isn't before the court, so there's no case number and I can't file a motion for discovery. The DNA taken from the crime scenes is in cold storage in Richmond, and I need a court order for Reliance DNA to have access, the private lab I hired."

"A court order or a favor," said Stackhouse. "Tomorrow you and I will forcibly ask for one. Considering our good-standing, and the high opinion of Mackenzie, we should get it."

Ronnie leaned her chin in her hand, and her posture surrendered a few inches. She was no longer eating. "I think so too. I issued a personal courier today with Mackenzie's skin and hair, so Reliance will already have it ready. They can clear him in less than twenty-four hours as soon as they have access."

"What if it doesn't?" said Timothy. "What if the lab results do not clear him?"

No one answered.

Timothy wiped his mouth. Set down his napkin. He picked up his fork but then placed it atop the napkin.

"Mackenzie, this is a ridiculous question. I know it is. But your profession has brought you into violence far more often than most men. Too much has been asked of you, even though each time you've come out alive and mostly unharmed. Some of the cases have intimately involved those of us in this room. If these men are dead because of you...would you trust us? Would you be able to admit it in front of your attorney and the sheriff?"

Fair question, said Kix. *Artfully phrased. Also, I am sorry but my rice has exploded onto the floor. If rice makes dogs sick, the time to act is now.*

"It wasn't me. And if it was, I would tell you," I said. "Without fear of consequence."

"Good. That's how it should be. You trust me with the truth. And I trust your word," he said. "So then, what happens if the DNA is yours?"

"I'll discover how it got there."

"Even if it's his DNA, that wouldn't be enough to convict Mackenzie of murder. Or even warrant an indictment. If the detectives tried, a grand jury wouldn't consider a true bill," said Ronnie.

"A true bill?"

"A formal charge. The grand jury would deny the detectives' request," said Ronnie.

"I did some poking today too. It's complicated as hell, because of all this." Stackhouse waved her hand to indicate the gathered assembly and the relationships. "But I learned a few things off the record. The police truly have no other suspects. No tips, no leads, no hunches, no persons-of-interest, nothing. They have only Mackenzie."

"Did you see the crime scene reports?" I said.

"No. That might be a fireable offense."

"Access to the victims' phones and computers would be helpful," I said. "Or a list of what the detectives took from each house."

"Until you're charged, that's a no-go."

"It's almost as if murderers shouldn't be investigating their own homicides," I said.

"You're not a murderer," said Timothy. "Or at least, you didn't kill these men."

The way he said it, it was a statement of trust, but also some validation would be welcome.

Listen, said Kix. His face was brown with soy sauce, and rice was stuck between his fingers, and he was looking at the floor. *This is your fault. If you'd like to bring me a warm washcloth, I'll do my best to help you clean up your disaster.*

"I'll give him a bath." Ronnie stood. "I can't eat anyway."

~

THAT NIGHT RONNIE swallowed a Zoloft and a Unisom, and she squeezed my hand tight.

"It's not that I don't trust your character, Mackenzie," she said. "And it's not that I don't trust your ability as an investigator, or have faith in myself as a defense attorney. It's only... I cannot imagine an investigation having higher stakes. Every year innocent men are jailed for crimes they didn't commit. A lot of innocent men."

She kissed me and fell asleep.

With that comforting thought, I didn't.

7

I bought coffee and two Bismarks from Dunkin Donuts and I took them to my office the next morning, in the company of Georgina Princess. Fortifications for the grueling work.

Ninety-seven persons named Torres lived in the Roanoke area. Thirty-three had phone numbers listed in the white pages online, and twenty-one of them answered my phone call. None of them knew a Donald Torres.

I found eighteen additional Torres on Facebook and I messaged them.

Sorry to intrude, but I'm doing research into the recent passing of a man named Donald Torres, who lived in Roanoke City. Did you happen to be family?

The answers rolled in throughout the day, all negative.

Everything was negative about Don Torres. I didn't have his social security number or birthdate, so my background checks weren't thorough, but I found no criminal record, no court record, no bankruptcy filing, no census data, no tax liens, no marriage license, no work history, no photos. The only concrete evidence I found that the man even existed was his property ownership.

It was impossible for a person to cover his tracks so thoroughly.

Which meant either I was missing something, or Donald Torres wasn't his real name. It was an alias. Or he'd legally changed his name.

"Ah *hah*," I said.

That's what bothered me at his house. I'd seen no personal effects. In the basement he had boxes of books and blankets and decorations, but no old tax documents, no family pictures, no childhood memorabilia, no journals. Nothing intimate, nothing about who he'd been the past forty-five years. Everything in that house could be purchased at a store in Roanoke, as though he arrived with nothing. Not even a name.

Starting over with a new identity was rare. Extremely rare. So was being beaten to death with a hammer. A correlation was all but guaranteed.

"The plot thickens," I told Georgina Princess. Through the window, the sun had laid down a warm spot on my floor, and that was where she stayed.

On the legal pad where I kept notes, I wrote that Donald Torres was NOT his real name, and I underlined NOT twice, and it made me feel like I'd gotten somewhere. Later on I'd dwell on this, but in the meantime...

Jason Hicks.

His identity was screamed at the cosmos.

I knew everything about him. Even his credit score, which was better than mine, and I resented it. Immediately after Roanoke College, he'd taken a job at RE/MAX, and three years later he switched to MKB, and eighteen months ago to Berry Realty Group. His realtor license was up to date. No criminal history. He owned his house, and a condo at Smith Mountain Lake which could be rented for three hundred a night. He ran the Drumstick Dash each Thanksgiving. He posted selfies of reaching the Seven Summits around the valley—he completed the challenge once a year, looked like, taking his brown Lab with him. He ate downtown a lot, often alone, sometimes with friends. Never married. No children. No public romances within the past six months.

Had Donald and Jason ever met?

I stood and stretched and wondered why I was stiff, and Georgina Princess said it had something to do with being alive forty years, and oh please oh please oh please could we go for a walk.

We did, and she found a spot of grass to do her business, thoroughly unashamed, even when I had to clean it up. Two women stopped to pet her and declare her a good dog. One of the women stayed too long to chat, and looked as though she thought the good dog had a good owner, and maybe I would ask her out.

Although I was technically married, I wore no wedding band.

Ronnie and I had fought through a world full of pain to be with one another, privately and legally joining in matrimony long before the fight was over, and when the dust settled I'd proposed with a diamond ring and the suggestion we start our matrimony with a public ceremony. She agreed.

And then life happened. Her ex-fiancé made himself intrusive again, and I took on cumbersome cases, and we'd gained a dog, Kix refused to leave for college, and her law firm demanded much of her, and we still had a Manny. Instead of a wedding ceremony, we existed in affectionate stasis. A lovely place to be, but I still wore no wedding band and remained in constant peril of female predation.

Maybe I'd buy myself one.

Mackenzie August, hopeless romantic.

GPA and I vacated downtown, and we drove to the house of the man who'd pretended to be Donald Torres. GPA stayed in the Honda and I knocked on doors.

The house directly to Donald's left, no one answered.

The woman who lived on the other said she'd already talked to the police and she'd never spoken a word to the dead guy, didn't even know his name, and he rarely came outside and she went to bed early and she saw nothing the night he was murdered. She worked as pharmacy tech for thirty years and she was retired now and she wished people would quit bothering her.

"But what if the man of your dreams comes knocking?" I said.

She glowered at me and closed the door. Which was, I thought, hurtful.

I tried the house directly across from Donald.

The curtain fluttered and a woman said, "I help you?"

I held up my badge and license.

The badge was new. Private detectives weren't required to carry them, but after years of encountering reluctance and suspicion I broke down and bought one. It looked similar to a detective badge—a gold shield—and I carried it in a wallet, along with the license. I didn't walk around with the PI wallet, only when I needed shock and awe. Flashing it felt hackneyed, like a prop. But it worked.

I told her my name and I was investigating the death of her neighbor.

A trim woman wearing black and pink workout gear

opened up. Her hair was cornrowed and her eyelashes were fake. A child was shouting somewhere behind her.

"You still haven't found the killer?" she said.

"Not yet. But it's only my second day."

"You're bigger than the other cops."

"Good breeding, is all."

"Do you know Archie?" she said.

"Sure I know Archie Hart."

"He's my cousin. Or like third cousin removed or whatever. You want to come in?"

I did and she closed the door, because it was breezy. Her house had the same layout as Don Torres'. We were in the television room. She wasn't a smoker.

"I don't know what else I can tell you. I said everything I know."

"Does the name Jason Hicks ring a bell?"

"Don't think so. Why?" she said.

"I'm not sure."

"That's a weird answer. My name's Imani, by the way."

"I'm Mackenzie."

"That's a real White name," she said.

"I couldn't be Whiter if I tried. Though my roommate is Puerto Rican."

"So?"

"Good point. Did Don ever have people over?"

"Does that matter?" she said.

"We don't know who killed Don." I used the royal We, like I was working with the cops, instead of being persecuted by them. "What we do is, we follow the threads of his life to the point the thread ends, and then pick a new thread, and eventually down one of the threads we run into the culprit. But we don't know which thread yet. It could be his social life."

"That's a big thing to say, Mackenzie. I'm going to steal it, but for other stuff."

"Be my guest. So, did Don have people over?"

"No," she said. "He was kinda boring."

"Did you two talk?"

"Sometimes I went for a jog, he'd be outside. We said hello. I told him welcome to the neighborhood once. He never came over. He never tried."

"When you encountered him, what was he doing outside?" I said.

"Mackenzie, I dunno."

"Working on the lawn?"

"Sure, something like that."

"Did he have a car?"

"Don't think so," she said.

"How'd he get around?"

She wrinkled her nose and looked over my head, like she knew the answer but she forgot. "The bus, maybe, I don't know."

"Do you know who found the body?" I said.

"I did."

"You did?"

"You didn't know that? They didn't tell you? You cops don't talk?" she said.

Embarrassing.

"I'm working two homicides right now, and I forgot. You can't be this good-looking and have a great memory," I said.

The crease between her eyebrows deepened.

"How'd you find him?" I said.

"Looked through the window."

"Why?"

"Why what?" she said.

"What made you look?"

"Brenda said she was worried."

"Who is Brenda?" I said.

"Mackenzie, you should talk to your cop friends, shouldn't you? About this?" She said it with a smile, like my incompetence made her feel good.

"I hate them," I said.

"I feel that. Brenda lives there." Imani pointed through the window at the house beside Don's. Brenda hadn't been home—I'd tried.

"Did Brenda know Don was dead?"

"No. She said she was worried. She said she hadn't seen him in a few days."

"Were she and Don friends?"

"No. She said she didn't know him either."

"Is Brenda nosey?" I said.

"No. She said..." Imani paused. "No wait. That's it. That's it, Mackenzie, my bad."

"What is?"

"Don didn't take the bus. Don took Ubers."

"He took Ubers?"

"You asked earlier why he was outside when I jogged and you asked how he got around. I forgot. I said the bus, but no, he took Ubers everywhere. And it was always that same guy, and when Don didn't call an Uber for two days, that same guy got worried and he asked Brenda if Don was okay, and then Brenda, she asked me."

"So the Uber guy first noticed Don was missing," I said.

"I think so. I didn't tell the police, though, cause I forgot."

"Maybe Brenda told them," I said.

"Maybe. But she's having a double bypass or something."

Behind her, the child began shouting louder. Calling for mom. Imani either couldn't hear it or didn't care. She was looking me over, like wondering if I'd ever used steroids.

"Did he take the Uber to work?" I said.

"I guess."

"What about to the store?"

"I guess," she said.

"Where did he work?"

"Mackenzie, I have no idea about that."

"Did he leave every day at the same time?" I said.

"Yup. Like nine or something. I leave for the gym at 9:30. I work there, you know."

"You said it was always the same Uber car."

"Yeah. You work out?" she said.

"I dabble."

"Looks like it. What'd you squat?"

"It's been a couple years since I squatted a lot of weight." I did some math. Oh...shoot. It'd been a decade. How the heck. "I was deadlifting over five hundred."

"You can't anymore?"

"No."

"Why not?"

"Because if I break my back, my kid will judge me," I said.

"I got a kid too."

"I know."

"I train, Mackenzie. You could come to Crunch," she said.

"If I catch Don's killer, I'll consider it."

The kid somewhere in the recesses of the house reached a new decibel. Still Imani took no notice.

I, however, would soon be deaf.

I said, "I'll locate Don's Uber driver and find out where he worked. I'll come back if I need to."

"You come back anytime, Mackenzie."

I left and she closed the door, but I could still hear the kid.

I returned to my car and the peace within and I said, "How does one summon an Uber?"

GPA yawned at me.

I found no local phone number, so I googled it. Google suggested I download an Uber App from the App store, and I did, but then I had to make an account. My thumbs were too girthy to be efficient on a phone and I cursed a lot, but eventually I had an Uber account.

Uber knew where I was already, and it asked me where I wanted to go. I didn't know. I guessed downtown. Uber presented a map and on the map it showed Uber cars driving around in real time. I knew exactly where each Uber car was in Roanoke. Looked like maybe ten. Did I want to confirm a ride?

"The robots," I said, "will soon kill us all."

GPA sighed about it.

I confirmed a ride, and Uber told me my car would arrive in six minutes.

Sure enough, six minutes later, a black Kia Rio braked by the curb. I bent down to speak to the driver through the window.

"Morning," I said.

"Good morning. Get in, please, sir." He was Middle Eastern. His face was round and stern, and his hair was thick and black, and he had scarring under his left eye.

"Weird question. Did you know Donald Torres?"

"What? Get in, please, sir."

"Do you know this house?" I pointed at Don's. "Did you frequently drive a man here?"

"What? No, sir. Are you ready, sir?"

"You've never been to this house?"

"No sir," he said.

"A man here often patronized Ubers. I need his driver."

"What?"

"I want the Uber driver who came to this house every day," I said.

"It wasn't me, sir. Do you need a ride, sir?"

"How do I find that particular driver?"

The guy gripped the steering wheel harder, probably to foreclose his desire to punch the idiot. "I don't know. It was not me."

"If I call for another ride, will Uber send you back here?" I said.

"Not if you don't want me, sir."

"I'd like to call for another ride. But not you. No offense."

I smiled, like—*you know how it is.*

"I will not accept it again, sir. Please leave me a good review sir, and I will not leave you a bad one."

"I don't know what that means, but I'll google it." I held out a twenty. "Thanks for your help."

"You already paid me, sir."

"The heck you say."

"What?"

"I didn't pay you."

"You did. When you called for me. I will be paid. Or..."

His eyes went vague. "Or…maybe I will? I do not know how… No one has canceled me before, sir."

"Take this. Don't come back."

"Yes sir." The man took the twenty and drove away, and I knew he was going to tell his friends about me being an idiot.

I summoned another Uber and waited seven minutes.

A woman arrived in a Hyundai Elantra.

Imani had said the driver was a guy. Not a woman.

I told the woman I needed to cancel, and I was sorry, and I gave her a twenty, and that I'd be calling for a different Uber in a minute and would she please not answer the summons, and she thought I was sexist and she took the money and she left.

I had sixty-five dollars left. How many calls would it take?

Four, was the answer.

The fourth guy braked next to me in a Chevy Tahoe and he turned down the hip-hop music, and I said, "Morning. Or…afternoon. Did you know Donald Torres?"

The driver wore wrap-around sunglasses and a big smile and he said, "Yeah, man, I know Don! How is he? Shit, man, like he dropped off the end of the whole world!"

"Did he frequently hire you?"

"Hell yeah he did. Thick as thieves. He reserved me every morning until one day he didn't."

According to the Uber app, this guy's name was Jordan. Based on Jordan's smile, and his hope that Don was okay, and shining unquestionable innocence, Jordan would not make my list of suspects.

"Jordan, I have bad news."

I told him.

Jordan jumped. The car lurched forward until he slammed the brake and put his Tahoe in park.

"Say that again?" said Jordan.

"I'm a private cop and I'm looking into his death."

"Oh shit, man. Oh *shit*, man. What happened?"

"Good question. Do you know where Don worked?" I said.

"Yeah, he worked at the collab. Downtown, you know? Took him there most days. He didn't like the other drivers. What happened to him?"

"A hammer."

"A hammer? *Shit*, a hammer."

"Here's what I want to do. I want you to drive me to his office and then drive me back here. Can you do that?" I said.

"Yeah, hell yeah, man. Get in."

I told GPA I'd be right back and I cracked the window. The day was cool, there was no danger, except to my seats if she needed to obey nature.

I climbed into the back of the Tahoe.

Onward progress.

8

Jordan was quick on the accelerator and hard on the brakes and aggressive on the hip-hop. Until we reached a red light and when it turned green Jordan kept staring off into nothing, shaking his head, and a car behind us honked.

Jordan barreled forward and he said, "Shit. I never known a man to die. A hammer? Got'damn, a *hammer*."

"Tell me where you drove him."

"The collab. That's about it. Sometimes to Aldi for groceries, sometimes to 7-Eleven." Jordan wore sunglasses but I could tell half the time he was watching me in the rearview.

"Who did he work for?"

"I don't know. Someone in that building, I guess? I'll show you the front. Something to do with money."

"How do you know, money?" I said.

"Don, he was my guy, right? My *guy*, we were friends. But he was always angry. Pissed off 'bout something, the whole damn day. Usually it was money. I say, how you doing, Don? And he'd say, I can't make enough money, Jordan, cause the world is full of *duraki*."

"*Duraki*."

"He was Russian or some shit. But he said that word a lot. *Duraki*. Told me it meant stupid people," said Jordan.

"Don was Russian."

"Something like that, yeah. Everybody is stupid, he said. Everybody but him. Or maybe it was only Americans."

I could see it now, based on Don's picture. He looked Russian or Eurasian, somewhere in that part of the world, where the anger and pride and the cold and the hard history produced hard faces.

"Tell me more about him."

"That's it, I swear to God. Man didn't talk much, except to complain about money and stupid people, but he tipped good. Oh, he liked Roanoke's traffic. Said there was no traffic here and it was nice."

"Do you know the name Jason Hicks?" I said.

Jordan said he didn't, and he braked on Church Avenue, in front of 16 West Market Place. A narrow street downtown, two blocks from my office.

"This is the place," said Jordan. "He walked in those doors and I drove away, and if I was still working that afternoon he'd reserve me again."

I knew the place, but I'd never been inside. It looked like a small shopping plaza, only a few stores.

I dropped a twenty onto the seat next to him and he drove me back to my car, a nine minute trip. He handed me his card and told me to text when I found out who killed his boy Don. The Tahoe roared away and the hiphop music cranked up, and I liked Jordan.

I let GPA out on a leash and she peed on one of

Donald's shrubs, and we returned to the city. I parked in front of my office and put her inside, where she had space to walk around and stick her nose out the window, and I walked the two blocks to 16 West Market Place.

The original building had been converted to a small gathering of shops with a common area. There was a salon, a coffee shop called Little Green Hive, an indie bookstore, apartments upstairs, and the collab area, which meant little offices for rent. The little open offices came with a desk and chair, and I assumed the internet and utilities were included. Perfect for the modern workforce of freelance mercenaries.

All the office spaces were vacant, except for an Indian woman near the front. I showed her my credentials and the photo of Donald and she pointed to a nearby desk.

I said, "Did you know him?"

She shook her head.

"Did you two ever speak?"

She shook her head. "Not once."

"Did he know anyone here?"

She shook her head again. Consistency. I thanked her.

Donald Torres' desk was empty, except for the little sign that said reserved. I saw no evidence of a police investigation. I sat in his chair and I pulled on latex gloves. The Indian woman watched without comment. I wondered if I looked guilty or if I looked like I was doing what cops did.

The top drawer contained stacks of papers. I found market studies and stock predictions. Printouts of Market Watch and Yahoo Business. Account statements, investment bumf, and a hand-drawn graph charting his progress, labeled in a language I didn't recognize. Could be Russian.

I had to guess, this looked like the work of a burgeoning stock-trader.

The bottom drawer was locked, but the desk was cheap and I slid a knife blade behind the drawer face until the lock clicked free. Inside I discovered a laptop. I removed it. No, two laptops. I removed the second. No, *three* laptops. Each of them a newish Dell XPS. I opened them all, but they were password protected.

I drummed my fingers.

How would Sherlock Holmes handle passwords?

He'd call Manny.

Manny answered on the third ring.

"I can't tell you what I'm doing, *amigo.*"

"I understand."

"But it involves a *pendejo* who used to be a good-looking game show host, and now he sells heroin to young girls and maybe I'll run him over."

"That was my guess," I said.

Someone spoke in the background.

Manny said, "Beck says that was too much information and I could be fired, but I think her skirt is too short today for her to be judging honest Americans."

"You two in the car?"

"The best car."

"I have three laptops I need unlocked. Could Beck handle that?" I said.

"She says her skirt is not too short and we shouldn't be looking. You think she's right?"

"Yes, *si, absolutamente*. And the laptops?" I said.

"You forgot your password."

"They aren't mine. And the owner is deceased," I said.

"This about the guys you forgot you murdered."

"One guy, I could understand forgetting. But two?"

"Seems unlikely." Manny put the phone down and I listened to the buzzing of muffled voices.

He came back.

"Beck can look at the computers tomorrow morning. I've seen her do it before. Like magic."

"*Gracias*. I'll text her the address," I said.

We hung up and I stared at the financial printouts and wondered if his murder had anything to do with these. And if so, why that involved me.

"Who killed you, Donald Torres," I said, and I packed up, and I took off my latex gloves. "And what's your real name."

I bought a coffee in the Little Green Hive and displayed a picture of Don, but neither barista had spoken to him, though they recognized the face. He'd always brought his own coffee, they said. I showed his picture at the Vintage Vault, but the woman said she'd never seen him before. I handed my card to the Indian woman at the front desk and told her that Donald Torres was dead, and that's why I was investigating, and her eyes widened at that—everyone's eyes widen—and she said she would call me, should the situation require it.

I fetched GPA and we drove to Jason Hicks' house. The second guy I murdered.

His family and the moving truck were gone. They'd cut the grass, though. I peered through the window at the front living room. One of the chairs had been taken, as had the television, making the room look barren and useless. Was it odd that the family brought a moving truck within the first seven days, and half-gutted the place? It was prompt, but was it suspicious?

I knocked on the doors of the neighbors, until a nice lady across the street invited me in. She was active and healthy but her spine had begun to stoop, the same way Ronnie's would in her advancing years, the same way mine would in prison. The lady wore a cardigan over a flowered turtleneck, and she wore wireless glasses, and her hair was permed. Her living room was full of knick-knacks that had no use, and the walls were hung with paintings of old trees and barns, I got the vague impression she liked to shop at places like Gatlinburg or Pigeon Forge for curios.

She had tea steeping in the kitchen and she poured me a little mug without asking, and I wondered if living in the fifties and sixties had been like this, with national manners instead of angst. A display case of decorative silver spoons was on the wall above the kettle.

"You're quite tall," she said.

"It's merely the strength of my character."

"I beg your pardon?"

"You knew Jason," I said.

"Yes, I knew Jason. He was the politest man. He shoveled my drive and my sidewalk after a snow. The city sends you nasty mail if you don't shovel your walk, you know."

I drank tea. It was bad. Tea's always bad.

"The politest man," she said again.

"We don't know why such a polite man was murdered. We're looking for any leads, no matter how innocuous," I said.

"We? Your license says private. Do you work with the police?"

"You don't miss much."

"I'm old." She smiled into her mug. "But I'm not senile. Not yet."

"I'm investigating it alongside the police. Anything I learn, I'll turn it over to them."

It was true.

It was mostly true.

"I don't know what to tell you, though."

"He wasn't dating anyone," I said.

"Not that I saw. You know young people have these programs that connect each other, for short-term trysts, and I cannot imagine anything more degrading. If Jason was dating, it was like that, and nothing serious or special."

"Did you see any girls over?" I said.

"A few months ago... No, it would have been last summer. He had a regular girlfriend then. But I go to bed earlier than I used to, and he was often out late. But the nicest man."

I brought up his pictures on Facebook and showed her the photo of Jason with a girl. Their last photograph was six months ago.

"Her?" I said.

"Yes, that's her. Maybe. We never spoke."

"What about friends?" I showed her another photo, Jason eating at a restaurant in a group. "Did any of these come over?"

"I don't know. Sweetheart, if I can be honest, you young men look alike."

"Even me?" I said. "With a likeness to Hercules?"

She indicated her own face and made a swirling motion. "I would remember you. You look as though people hit you quite a bit."

"I used to look like Robert Redford."

"Oh honey." She patted my arm. "Nobody looks like Robert Redford."

I drank more tea and regretted it.

"Jason's friends. Were they over much?"

"Yes, some. They would grill on Jason's rear porch and play music. They liked modern country music," she said.

"But you wouldn't recognize them."

"No. To be honest, I assume poor Jason was murdered by one of them. I have no reason to suspect those boys, other than I don't know who else it could be. It's a scary thing, sleeping across from a crime scene. I ordered an alarm system, but it won't be installed until next week."

I set my card on the table and said, "If you hear something at night, call me."

"That's awfully sweet of you. I usually call my son. He says I should get a dog. But a dog didn't help Jason, I tell him. That's how we knew to call the police."

"The dog?" I said.

"A Labrador named Brownie. Brownie started howling. I tell you, just a'howling. We heard it through the walls. Mr. French across the street checked first, and he called 911."

I thanked her for the tea and told her I would talk to Mr. French next.

"He's a dentist," she said. "He won't be in until after dinner, and don't bother calling his ex-wife."

"I probably will."

"Why?" she said.

"Because good investigators do the work."

"And bad investigators?"

"Bad investigators pin crimes on guys they shouldn't, because it's easier that way," I said.

"That's a cynical way to view the world, Mr. August."

"It's been a week."

9

I was sitting at the desk of Donald Torres the next morning when Noelle Beck arrived. Her hair was up in a bun and she wore a blue pants suit. I reflected a moment on how she'd changed since I first met her—the pants and shirt were snug instead of loose, obviously tailored to her measurements, and she wore makeup now, and her hair was forever up in a bun but it looked healthy and shiny and tangle-free. Either she'd matured and realized she could be attractive without compromising her professionalism, or she'd made these changes so Manny would leave her alone.

She placed a heavy bag on the desk, next to Donald's three computers, and said, "For the record, my skirt was not too short."

"I doubt that's even possible."

"Manny is always complaining that my skirts are too long. So I bought a shorter one, and now he...ugh."

"How much of our lives," I said, "are lived in a such a way as to avoid his wrath?"

"I made the mistake of drinking a Pepsi around him last week."

"Dear Lord."

She began ticking her fingers. "For starters, it should be Coke, not Pepsi. Second, I was betraying my faith with the caffeine. Third, that much sugar? *No bueno*. Fourth, was I aware of the diabetes associated with high fructose corn syrup? If I must, it should be pure cane. Fifth, it would make me too jittery. Sixth, what about my macros? And had I considered my image? Did I think single guys would be intrigued by the girl pounding sodas?"

"Rookie mistake."

"I didn't get work done for at least thirty minutes, listening to the diatribe."

I stood so she could sit.

"Thank you for the help," I said.

"I'm sure you know, but anyone who's heard about this believes you're innocent." She snapped on gloves. "Plug the laptops in, please?"

I found a power strip and charging chords in the large drawer. An outlet was built into the floor, so I connected the laptops to it.

Beck had brought two computers—one PC and one MacBook. Because Donald had Dells, she opened her PC, a Lenovo. She connected hers to one of Donald's with an ethernet cable and she explained we would crack the passcode with a dictionary attack.

I nodded my understanding.

She smiled, typing. "It's a program that feeds common words and phrases into a lock-screen. People should use two-factor authentication but no one does. People should use a complex password, with multiple words and letters and symbols, perhaps fifteen digits long, but again no one does. Manny's is short and includes a pop star."

"Jennifer Lopez."

"You know his password," she said.

"No but I know Manny. And he says she's a top-five import from Puerto Rico."

"Ah hah," she said. "That was easy."

Donald Torres' screen blinked, and his Windows desktop appeared. Unlocked.

"Wow."

"ABC123!! Embarrassing." Noelle tried the password on the other two computers, each of which unlocked immediately. "You're in."

"You have magical powers."

"Let's see..." Noelle opened an Explorer browser and looked at his history to find his email server. As she worked, she made a soft clicking noise at her front teeth. "It appears he saved his passwords. His Hotmail is ready for your inspection."

"Thanks."

"No problem."

"Why do you think he uses three laptops?"

Noelle stood. She picked up the financial printouts and skimmed them. "Just a guess. He wants extra screens but he's not savvy enough to connect multiple monitors to a single hard drive."

"Why would he want extra screens?"

"He's into money, and he wants to watch stocks in real time. He could be jumping into and out of the market constantly. I don't know a lot about day trading, but I know more screens are better." She tugged off the gloves and shot them into a nearby trash can. "Good luck,

Mackenzie. Please let me know if I can help again. It's an honor, after all the ways you and Ronnie have helped me."

She packed and left, like she had somewhere to be, and probably did, and I wondered what possible influence Ronnie and I had in her life.

I tried utilizing Donald's track pad with my gloves on, but it was useless, so I took them off and set a reminder on my phone to wipe the laptops down later. Eventually Detective Green would learn about this desk—I'd tell him myself—and there was no reason for my prints to be here.

Each of the computers had a simple browsing history.

Computer One was used for Interactive Brokers, TD Ameritrade, and a website called RobinHood, for buying and selling stocks at a moment's notice. This machine moved money.

Computer Two was used for Reddit pages, including WallStreetBets, and Investopedia and Bloomberg, for research into up-to-the-minute trends. While he watched his money move, he wanted to read about it, and he used this second machine to do it.

Day trading was a world that eluded me. I was as adept at it as I was at building the descent stage of a moon rocket, but I could read dollar amounts and it appeared Donald Torres was moving around tens of thousands of dollars. I browsed the Ameritrade records and consulted a printout—the Dow had jumped three percent last month, and he'd made twenty-six grand.

Computer Three was used for the other things—word processing, YouTube, Wordle, Wikipedia, ESPN, Amazon, and email.

His email drew me first.

I read and scrolled, read and scrolled. In the past few

months, his inbox was as it should be—notes from his bank, spam, confirmation for online purchases, bills, ESPN updates (he was a Yankees fan, gross), financial newsletters, Reddit alerts, itinerary reminders from Travelocity, and marketing emails from frequented unsavory websites.

I worked through the travel itinerary—he was scheduled to fly to Beirut next month. A room was reserved at the Mövenpick Hotel. No return flight had been booked.

"Leaving for good, Donald?" I said.

The volume of incoming emails decreased the farther back I went, until a year ago his inbox was nothing but forwards from an unfamiliar address. This made sense; Donald Torres had begun a new life and the forwards were from himself in his old life. If he was thorough, he'd forwarded these vital emails and then deactivated the old account. The emails contained bank information and important phone numbers and addresses, and a copy of his passport...

Hey-o!

I zoomed in on the passport image, his big hairy face. It was him.

Donald's real name was Danil. Danil Turgenev.

From Danil Turgenev to Donald Torres. Not a great leap.

Jordan had been correct—Donald was Russian. I wondered if he had an accent. I didn't think to ask Jordan about it.

I took photos of everything with my phone.

He had sent himself multiple addresses and phone numbers. I looked them up on a browser. Three addresses in Brooklyn, two in Newark. I called the phone numbers. One was disconnected, one went to an unlabeled voice mail, and one sounded as though a fax machine tried to pick up.

If I had to formulate a hypothesis on the spot, I'd hypothesize that Danil Turgenev had angered someone in the Russian mafia and fled New York to start over, relationships and ties thoroughly severed. His only asset being money, he swelled it through day trading, a hard thing to track. Now he had enough to move to Beirut.

It was flimsy. And probably I'd missed points, but it was all I had.

Kix would ask if I was talking about sex.

I read until there was nothing else. I took screenshots of certain emails, then I wiped my prints off the computers, put the gloves on, and returned the machines to the drawer.

A Russian with ties to New York, starting life afresh in Roanoke under a different name, gets himself beaten to death by an as-yet unknown killer, and the DNA of Mackenzie August is found under his nails.

A predicament sure to bamboozle lesser detectives.

Then again, lesser detectives got themselves into fewer predicaments.

10

I sat at a light, exiting downtown on Franklin, and one of Jason Hicks' friends called me, and I put it on speaker.

"Hi, yeah, this is Officer August?"

I was not an officer of the law. And the insinuation rankled.

"You bet," I said.

"This is Geoff Patton. I got your message. About Jason Hicks?"

"Geoff Patton." He was one of the guys eating dinner with Jason a few months ago, memorialized with a photograph on Facebook. I didn't know which one, though. He had floppy hair. They all did.

"I guess the killer hasn't been caught yet?"

"I don't appreciate your tone, Geoff."

"Oh. Oh, damn, my bad," he said.

"This is a weird one, Geoff. Cops usually have their man within the first forty-eight hours, or they're close. It's been over a week and we're neither. I'm looking in new places," I said.

"Well, I was in Blacksburg that night. With Ezra and Hazel. So it wasn't me."

"Ezra and Hazel."

The best detectives repeat stuff.

I remembered the name Ezra.

"Yeah, Ezra said you called him, I thought?"

"Someone did. We know it's not you, Geoff," I said, though I knew nothing of the sort, and I was making liberal use of the royal We again. "I want to run through this one more time. Sound good? Tell me how you knew Jason."

"Roanoke College. He's from here. Roanoke, I mean, but I guess you know that? I transferred in from Emory & Henry, and Jason was the first guy who gave a damn about me. We both majored in Business Administration. I stayed after graduation, but listen, I really was in Blacksburg. There are witnesses. Jason said he wasn't going, so we left. I mean, we couldn't have known what would happen, right?"

"Left where?" I said.

"What?"

"Jason didn't want to go, and you left. Left where?"

"Sidewinders."

"Country bar downtown," I said.

"Right. Line dancing was over, but Hazel wanted to party with a guy in Blacksburg."

"Jason was at Sidewinders the night he died?"

"I thought you knew. Ezra didn't tell you?" he said.

"Just running through the facts again. You and Ezra and Hazel were with Jason Hicks at Sidewinders, and then you three left and Jason stayed."

"Right. When we heard Jason died, of course we

suspected that brunette, but Magnolia said they didn't leave together. You knew that?"

"I'll ask the questions, Geoff," I said.

"Oh, shit, sorry, man."

"What the hell kinda name is Magnolia?"

"Right, my bad, her real name's Piper, ahh, Piper West," he said.

I turned on my signal and parked illegally on the side of Main Street, so I could focus. Geoff was spewing a lot of weird names and facts.

I closed my eyes.

"Magnolia was at Sidewinders. And Magnolia told you Jason Hicks didn't leave with the brunette."

"That's right."

"Who is the brunette?" I said.

"I don't know, sir. None of us knew. They hit it off, line dancing. Some chick."

"Jason was dancing with some brunette chick," I said.

"They didn't leave together though."

"Because you talked to Magnolia later and Magnolia said they didn't."

"Her real name's Piper," he said.

"Magnolia didn't go to Blacksburg."

"No."

"Why not?" I said.

"Because she tends bar at Sidewinders. You didn't know... I mean, yeah, bartender."

"Magnolia tends bar and saw Jason talking to a brunette, but leave without her. She told you this."

"You got it," he said.

"Tell me her words. I'll call her later, but tell me exactly what Magnolia said."

"Ahhh... Damn, what if I get it wrong?"

"Do your best, Geoff. You think I'm a monster?"

"When I heard Jason was dead, I called Mags and said something like, Oh God, that brunette killed him, but Mags said, No way, the girl left an hour before him. And I said, Oh, and she said, Yeah Jason said he thought he was doing well but she got tired and went home."

"Had you seen the brunette before?" I said.

"No, first time. Mags didn't know her either. None of us did. But, it was just some girl he danced with and then it was over, sounds like, right? It happens."

It did happen. A lot.

But murders didn't.

"Maybe Magnolia was jealous of the brunette," I said.

"Mags? I doubt it. She's married. To a woman."

"Ah." Swing and a miss. "Tell me about Jason's love life."

"See, that's the thing. There wasn't one. Not since Luna," he said.

"The names of you people," I said.

"What?"

"Luna was his girlfriend. They broke up last summer."

"She moved to Oregon," he said.

"And Jason hadn't dated anyone since."

"No. That's why we were hyped about the brunette, sir."

"Cute girl?"

"Hell yeah. Magnolia thought so, too. She looked really into him. But..."

"But she got tired and left, and an hour later Jason did too," I said.

"That's what I know."

"Take your best guess. Who killed Jason?"

"Damn. I can't do that, sir."

"Try," I said.

"Nobody wanted to kill Jason. The nicest guy you ever... Like I said, he saved me at Roanoke College. Almost too nice, you know what I mean? Maybe his neighbor?"

"Why his neighbor?"

"I don't know. You said guess. Isn't it always the neighbor?"

"Do you know Donald Torres?" I said.

"Who?"

"Big swarthy Russian guy, Donald Torres."

"No. Should I?"

"Great question. I don't know," I said.

"Jason knew a lot of people. Maybe he sold Donald a house? He sold a ton."

"No, I checked. Good thinking, though, Geoff."

"Thanks." Geoff sounded pleased with himself, and he should be.

I told Geoff I might call him back later, and I phoned Sidewinders for Magnolia and she answered. A direct, fast-talking woman, she told me the same story Geoff did, adding that the brunette was shortish, trim, maybe too trim, good teeth, and when I pushed for more information she said the hair could've been a wig.

"A wig?" I said.

"A girl can tell. I'm not saying it was a wig, but I wouldn't be surprised. It was a little too shiny, a little too perfect, you know?"

"I don't."

"I forgot to tell the police about the wig. I forgot until now. Maybe a wig, maybe not. Maybe she just came from the stylist and I'm a bitch. Cute girl, not a great dancer, good at flirting though. But she left and I haven't seen her since," said Magnolia.

"Did she come alone?"

"I don't remember. Girls usually don't. We love Jason and we only noticed her because of him. *Loved* Jason, I guess. No. No, we love him still."

"Does Sidewinders have video cameras?"

"Yeah but you guys said it didn't help," she said.

"You guys?"

"The other officers. The cameras point at the bar, and there was no good view of the brunette girl. And again, she took off. He stayed here drinking with me."

"Who would want to kill Jason?"

"Nobody. Absolutely no one. Seems to me you boys will figure out he fell and hit his head and died that way, because Jason was Roanoke's most upstanding citizen," she said.

That wouldn't explain my DNA.

I DROVE to Kix's school and took him home.

We arrived minutes after Ronnie. The engine of her little red Mercedes was still clicking.

She stood in the kitchen, not moving, staring through the big rear window over the sink. Her arms were crossed and her spine was straight as a lightning rod.

I set Kix on the ground, near his toys in the corner.

"What's afoot?"

"I hung up with Reliance DNA," she said. "They rushed the results. The hair and skin samples scraped from the victims' nails? They're yours."

"My DNA." Icy tingles spread out from my spine, like frost.

"Your DNA. The police lab was right. I had been so

convinced they erred. Mackenzie," she said. "What are we going to do?"

"We're going to get a drink. We're going to talk. And we're going to not panic."

We did our best. Two out of three wasn't bad.

11

Ronnie and I sat on the front porch.

The evening had turned warmer than the day, somehow bringing the lights closer, the people closer, like the heat created a little world in which strangers could be friends. Windsor Avenue was a street crowded with ancient austere trees and big houses, and tonight cars drove slower and pedestrians tossed us waves.

"Mackenzie. I feel better," said Ronnie.

"Good."

"I panicked."

"Hard to blame you," I said.

"Panic is easier when you're obsessed with yourself, and I was. It is you being ambushed by the detectives, not me, and yet somehow I couldn't see beyond my own needs and my wants. My pulse has settled and I'm thinking clearly again, enough to see that was a very unhelpful panic attack, and I apologize."

"It wasn't a true panic attack," I said. Despite the idyllic temperature, we were under a blanket on the swing. "It was a darling tantrum."

"I acted like a fucking coward."

"A fit of passion."

"I nearly fainted, for God's sake," she said.

"I've been having minor episodes too. A few seconds of it now and then."

"I've been through a lot, and somehow this absurd episode makes me go weak in the knees. Also I'm sorry for saying fuck. Twice."

"I don't care the words you use, Ronnie."

"You were framed."

"That's what I think," I said.

"It's unthinkable. It's egregious. I've been a defense attorney for over ten years, and personally I have never worked with someone framed for...*anything*, much less murder, and the cases I've read, it was an amateurish, bumbling thing, easily disproved. This is beyond the pale, Mackenzie."

"The nature of the crime makes it easier to narrow down the culprit, though."

"I'm not involved in the early stages of a crime scene. Could a police officer plant the evidence?" she said.

"In this case, it's doubtful. The bodies were discovered by neighbors, and most likely multiple cops and medics entered the house in succession. I'll know for sure if I ever see the report."

"Either way, the perpetrator knows you. One doesn't frame a stranger so thoroughly."

"Yes," I said.

"And the person hates you."

"Hard to imagine. Or they stand to gain by my fall from grace," I said.

"How so?"

"For example, they could be in love with you. With me out of the picture..."

"You'll never be out of the picture, Mackenzie. But I see what you mean," she said.

"Revenge is the likeliest option. Ergo, at the moment that's my focal point."

"Someone who wants revenge, and has access to your DNA," she said.

"Not many do."

"It's Manny."

I nodded. "He found out the new silverware was made in the Philippines."

"Oh dear." She smiled.

Ronnie's smile set off cameras. The smile she reserved for me was a Duchenne brilliant smile, where her lips raised and peaked, showing perfect teeth and the hint of pink gums, and the corners curled. Manny said she smiled like the girl from the *Alias* show, a great American program.

"For the sake of argument," I said, "let's assume it wasn't him."

"Who else has access to your DNA?"

"It was my skin and hair."

"That's what the lab told me," she said.

"Did they mention how fresh the skin was, taken from under the fingernails?"

"No. I'll ask, but I don't know how determinative that will be."

"It's Helga," I said.

"*Helena*, and it can't be her. The DNA was planted—"

"I know it can't be her. I was being riotous."

Underneath our blanket, her toes were poking my shoe. Made me wish I was barefoot, though I never was.

I'd wear shoes in the shower if it wasn't ungenteel. "Is your office cleaned? The DNA could be lifted from your office chair?" she said.

"It's not cleaned, but that's an idea worth investigating. Breaking into my office however would leave evidence of damage."

"In the recent weeks, were you forced to wrestle wicked malfeasants?" she said.

I'd already gone through this process, but I did it again, out loud with her, in case I missed something.

"There's been no physical contact of late with wicked malfeasants. Potentially my DNA could've been taken from our train ride through the Rockies," I said.

"Yes. Carla had a key to our room."

"Carla's in jail, so let's cross her off the list. Before that, there was the big Homer Rose case, and he tried to wrestle me, but he's still in Alaska. I checked. Do you remember when I was hired to keep Roland Wallace alive? The old guy in the huge house? I was in and out quite a bit, and any number of people could've examined the collar of my jacket."

"Angelina, and Walter Lowe the private detective, and what's-his-name."

"Alan Anderson, the accountant. Those three are also still in jail."

"Mackenzie. It's remarkable how many people meet you and head directly to prison," she said and she squeezed my arm, and I flexed, she nearly fainted again. "There are too many suspects."

"There are."

"You already knew this," she said.

"Yes."

"You're letting me catch up."

"I'm not being patronizing. Talking it through helps," I said.

"What's next?"

"Cross-referencing people who had access to my hair with people who hate me, with people who are vicious enough to kill someone, with people who are smart enough to frame me and get away with it."

"Those are stringent filters," she said.

"It doesn't leave many people."

"Does it leave anyone?"

"Your ex-boyfriend, the Italian Prince, for one. I broke his shoulder and cost him the tournament in Naples, and he's smart, and he's a killer."

"He is not my ex-boyfriend. And framing you isn't his style."

"What do you mean?" I said.

"He would make a spectacular display of your death. Although he would perish in the attempt."

"Yes. He would."

"Mackenzie, it's almost as though the killer knows he couldn't beat you face-to-face, so he has to strike at you from a distance."

"Or she," I said.

"It's *not* Helena, Mackenzie."

"They can't beat me face-to-face, but I doubt it's a shooter, either. Otherwise, striking from a distance would be easy."

"So..." said Ronnie. "The person has to pass those stringent filters, and be weak in combat, and have no marksmanship."

"If the person knows me well then he or she knows about Manny, and knows that getting both of us would be damn-near impossible. Get one of us, miss the other, your life is forfeit. And a final filter, I think one of the victims, Donald Torres, had mob connections."

"Do you know that conclusively?"

"No," I said.

"Assuming the mob connection is real and germane, why Jason Hicks?"

"Good question, counselor."

"The killer might be a rich person who has hired someone else," she said.

"It could easily be that."

"We're not getting anywhere, are we," she said.

"We are. We're walking forward through the fog. Progress is progress."

"Is this progress?"

"At the minimum, we aren't doing nothing," I said.

She leaned her head onto my shoulder. "What next? As an officer of the court, there isn't much else I can do at the moment."

"At the moment, I don't need an officer of the court. I need the opposite."

"What's the opposite?" she said.

"A dirty rotten scoundrel."

LATER THAT NIGHT, I drove to Marcus Morgan's house. It was better than mine. It was obviously better, but in unapparent ways. I think because so many professionals had practiced their arts on it. The lighting was professional, the painting was fresh and professional, the mulch, the flowers, none of it looked like a hack job. Whereas, on Windsor, we just did our best.

Also he had tall planters with little Japanese maples. Only true ballers have tall planters.

He answered the door because I'd told him I was coming. He was dressed in black evening slacks and a black T-shirt with silver embroidered embellishments, and he wore reading glasses. I'm sure it was a coincidence, but they looked like the reading glasses Stringer Bell wore.

"August."

"It's warm tonight. Want to sit on your porch?" I said. "I'm great at that."

"You don't get to sit on my porch, honky. Let's walk my dog."

"That better not be innuendo."

He disappeared into his house. A rich aroma drifted out. Expensive incense. He returned carrying a tiny animal. He set it down, holding onto its leash.

"The hell," I said, "is that."

"This is Kittens."

"It's a kind of mouse?"

"It's a dog, motherfucka. French bulldog."

"But it's named Kittens," I said.

I nudged the animal with the toe of my shoe. It fell over. Got up. Smiled at me.

"Want to marry the woman you love?" said Marcus. "Sometimes she a crazy-ass psycho. And she names dogs stupid shit."

"Is Kittens a boy animal or a girl animal?"

"Don't think Kittens decided yet. We don't enforce gender stereotypes."

"Oh," I said.

"You think I'm serious."

"I don't judge," I said.

"Kittens is a girl. In the Morgan house, you be the gender you were born. Life's hard enough, ask me. My boy can barely dress himself. Fact he can't. How's he gonna make bigger decisions? Shit." He said the last word like sheeeit. We walked his driveway and down the sidewalk leading from his house, which sat on the crest of Wasena's tallest hill. We walked slow, else Kittens would drag and bounce. He lived on a cul-de-sac, quiet, little traffic. "Been a while. Was hoping you got your act together."

"I've been taking my ease. And I haven't seen you at church."

"We trying to be Baptist now. Episcopals..." He made an unhappy sucking sound at his teeth. "They're getting too liberal."

"You're sounding like a very conservative cocaine lord tonight."

"Gravity is gravity, even if you pretend it don't exist. Even if you call it something else, like a lollipop, gravity still kick your ass. You ask me, church shouldn't be dancing around to the tune of whatever the culture says, cause the culture is a fuckin' disaster, so why the hell we listening to it? Gravity's gravity, and truth is truth, and the Bible is the Bible, and God is God, and boys are boys, and everything else is pretend, and I don't have time to pretend so people can not get their fake-ass feelings hurt, got'damn it. Anyway." A deep breath at the stars. "You know what's funny? The Black community, we some of the most conservative people in America. Outside of California, that is. Look it up. It's true. So why the hell are White liberal women the ones loud about Black issues?"

"Um," I said.

"Black lives matter, but our opinions don't?"

"Perhaps I came on a bad night? You watching cable news a lot?"

"Naw. I digress. My wife says I need to talk less about it." Kittens stopped at a mailbox. Sniffed it and peed on it. I assumed. The animal was so small I couldn't really tell what it was doing. "What'cha want, August. You didn't come to pay respect, that's obvious."

"I came for the sermon."

"Up yours."

"Did you know Donald Torres?" I said.

"No."

"What about Danil Turgenev?"

"No. Sounds Russian."

"He was," I said. "Same guy, different name."

"You kill him?"

"Maybe, but I doubt it."

"The hell's that mean?"

"The Kings don't have much to do with Russians," I said.

"No. D.C. down to Miami, it's Latinos and Blacks. Above that, it's Russian and Italian. Some Irish too. We don't play well."

"But the leader of the Kings is a White woman."

"Don't tell nobody. It's embarrassing."

"So you wouldn't know if a Russian mafia guy moved here? And you wouldn't care if he was murdered?" I said.

"I would not. I need to know, someone would tell me. You want me to find out?"

"He was murdered and I'm being framed for it. I want to know if it's mafia related."

"Why mafia? Lotta people hate you."

"Because he came here from New York, I think, and

started over with a new identity," I said. "Like he was hiding from powerful persons."

"Didn't hide good enough. What's it got to do with you?"

"No idea. Someone planted my skin and hair under his nails."

He grinned, a pearly crescent. "Kinda funny."

"It will be, later. At the moment, I'm irate."

"Don't look it," he said.

"Irate but stoic. Ask your contacts. Use my celebrity to inveigle them," I said.

"The heck's inveg-whatever mean?"

"Persuade through flattery."

"Yeah, that's it, August, I'll persuade the Kings though flattery to give up their secrets."

"Remind them that I am their Gabbia Cremisi champion," I said.

"Current champion is Japanese."

"That tournament is ongoing?"

"Every year. You thought you brought the whole thing down, didn't you."

"After me, I assumed they saw no reason to continue. Diminishing returns."

He turned toward home. "Kittens is done. We going home. I'll ask around."

"I appreciate it."

"Don't know why I suffer you."

"Me and Kittens, apex predators. Powerful allies," I said.

"Mostly I just clean up y'all's messes."

"That's hurtful."

12

The Roanoke City Police Station was on the same street as my office, Campbell Avenue. Though only five blocks removed, they were lengthy blocks and it felt a world apart. Like most stations, it was designed so people didn't want to be there, like a polished anvil to crash against. The floor was flecked tile, easier for squeegeeing blood. The walls were decorated with flags and wooden plaques, nothing breakable. The chairs were plastic, simple to spray down and clean. Abandon all hope, ye who enter.

Two parents sat whispering and sniffling with their son in the corner while a cop waited with thumbs tucked behind his utility belt.

The officer behind the broad desk, guy named Harden, had a slab-sided face to match the decor. He had a whisky nose too.

He said, "Hey, August, whaddaya say."

"You don't have to be nice. I didn't bring donuts."

"I'm low carb now anyway."

"Well, Harden. It shows," I said. It did not show. "Your uniform looks like a boy wearing a circus tent."

"I haven't lost a pound and I'm angry as a castrated bull, August."

"Yikes. Detective Green in?"

He took a breath and I heard it whistle through his nostrils. Then another, watching me with dead watery eyes.

"You sure, August? What I hear, maybe you shouldn't," he said.

Harden'd heard I was a suspect. The suspect. By now, most folks knew. Maybe every folk.

"Fortune favors the foolish, Harden," I said.

"Your funeral." He raised a phone and spoke into it, and two minutes later Detective Green opened a side door.

His khakis were flat-front and his white button-down shirt was tucked in, and he wore suspenders. Suspenders!

"Mack August." He stood in the doorway, hand on the knob.

"Green."

"You need to talk to me?"

"Better you than Captain Keto at the desk," I said.

Little beads of sweat glinted along Green's hairline.

"You understand there's no immunity being offered here. You say something stupid, I can use it."

"I have never," I said, "said something stupid."

He shoved the door wider and turned back into the offices and I followed, and the door closed heavy behind. The open bullpen, where resource officers, and patrol officers, and victim advocates, and evidence technicians had desks for their computers and paperwork, bustled. The air felt blue with sweat and smoke. Green didn't rank a closed office yet; those were reserved for the chief of police and his captains. Green's desk was in a covey of cubicles with other detectives, a little community to themselves.

I was watched by everyone.

Green probably gave daily updates to his lieutenant, who reported to the captain, who reported it to the chief. On top of that, Stackhouse and Ronnie had both been in here, calling on favors and shouting demands. I was essentially a minor celebrity falling from grace.

Green snatched his phone from his desk and we walked into an open conference room along the far wall. He saw his reflection in the glass and he fixed his hair, which was shiny with gel. Wiped his hands on his pants. I followed and I closed the door first so he couldn't.

Small victories.

Standing beside a chair, he took a deep breath to puff out his chest.

"Man-to-man, August, I don't know this is wise."

"I have never," I said, "not been wise."

"You don't want your attorney."

"Don't tell her I was here. She's under the impression I'm incautious."

He pointed at the chair opposite his. I sat. He sat.

"You should record this," I said.

"I am." Green placed the iPhone on the table and pressed record. "Of course."

In response, I set my own phone out and pressed record.

He sniffed. "Being cute?"

"I am never," I said, "not cute."

"What's on your mind, Mackenzie August?" he said.

"This is in regard to the homicides of Donald Torres and Jason Hicks."

"Okay."

"I'm here to trade information," I said.

"I'm not trading a thing. I won't divulge my investigative findings."

"You don't know what I want yet. Mostly I'm here to educate you, Green."

"Educate me," he said.

"I'd have this case solved by now, except you cleaned out the crime scenes and won't let me look at your reports. I'll give you what I have, and maybe you can assemble some puzzle pieces."

"I can assemble the puzzle pieces."

"I said maybe you could. My confidence isn't high."

"You know how weird this is, August? This is weird as hell. You're a known commodity around here. It's almost like you're famous but none of us knows why. Everybody likes you," he said.

"Do you?"

"No I don't like you."

"Rats. I got the one guy," I said.

"Now you're a suspect in two homicides and you show up running your mouth and being glib. August. I'm the lead on this and it's like you're trying to piss me off. You're looking at prison. You're looking at *life*."

"I'm looking at a man who doesn't have a clue," I said.

"What you're doing is, you're trying to get under my skin so I'll make a mistake, but it won't work."

"I didn't do this, Green. It looks like I did on the surface, but any detective worth his bullets would realize I wouldn't beat two people to death and leave them in their homes with my DNA. An idiot would do that, and I'm not one."

He didn't say anything.

"Donald Torres isn't his real name. You didn't know that, I presume," I said.

"What?"

"Donald Torres. It's a recently assumed identity."

"What do you mean?"

"You didn't know. I hoped you would. It would be a sign of competence," I said.

His phone rang. He looked at the caller ID. Grabbed it and stood and stepped out of the conference room and closed the door.

He paced the window, not looking in. The call was about me. He listened and nodded and listened and spoke, looking everywhere but at Mackenzie August, his primary suspect. Uniformed officers at their desks watched him and then me.

The call concluded and he checked his hair in the door window's reflection and he returned. He set the phone down and wiped his hands again and began recording.

"Okay. What's Donald's real name?" said Green.

"Donald Torres' real name is Danil Turgenev. He's Russian." I picked up my phone and pushed buttons. "I'm texting you his passport."

Green's phone buzzed and he swiped the screen a few times. Zoomed in on the photo I sent him. From his shirt pocket, he took out reading glasses and pushed them onto his nose.

"Looks like the guy," he said.

"What came back when you ran Donald Torres' fingerprints?"

"Nothing." Then he winced, because he'd given me information. He zoomed in on the passport's identifying details. "I'll be honest, August, I didn't know this."

"That is apparent," I said. "Painfully."

"Not sure this helps your case, your intimate knowledge of the victim."

"It didn't bother you that Donald didn't have a car? Or a history? Or a job?" I said.

"Sure it did. I even asked the Marshals if he was in witness security. The bus driver said he'd seen Donald on the bus, and that's why we didn't chase a car."

"You assumed you had your man, me, and that's why you didn't chase the car angle. Ever heard the term due diligence?"

"Don't be an ass in here, huh."

"Due diligence means the minimum. It doesn't mean thorough, it means the minimum. And you haven't even done that. It took me twenty minutes to find out Donald rode the bus some, but he took Ubers more. The same driver, almost always. Guy named Jordan who took me to Donald's office, where it's obvious that Donald traded stocks in his new life. I think he was running from the Russian mob."

"How do you know?"

"Because I don't suck at my job. Green."

"Dammit, August."

"Don't be sad. I'm just good at this."

"Where's his office?" he said.

"Does it hurt, asking questions to which you should've had the answer to weeks ago?"

I was punchy. No one could blame me.

"August. Where'd he work?"

I told him about the collab office space and the desk with the drawer and the computers and the emails. I didn't tell him the lock-screen passcode, so he'd have to come back and beg for that later.

Larger victories.

"So, what's the history with Danil Turg-whatever?" he said.

"That's what I want in return. I gave you Danil Turgenev, now I want you to use your resources to find out more. FBI, NCIC, whatever database you can. Call organized crime in Brooklyn, and tell me what you discover."

He held out his hands, like—*what do you want from me?*

"August, I cannot divulge—"

"—cannot divulge your investigative findings. But, you nincompoop, this wasn't your investigative finding. It was mine."

"I can't make any promises."

"You know about the brunette?" I said.

"Who?"

"The girl Jason Hicks danced with."

"Yeah I know about her. Couldn't get a good look at her face," he said.

"You didn't try very hard. Because you think you already have your man. But you don't. Which is why you're dropping evidence. You know she might've been wearing a wig?"

"A wig?"

"It's fake hair," I said.

"I know what a wig is."

"Used to be called a periwig. Or peruke? Ring any bells?"

"Shut up. How do you know she wore a wig?"

"I asked questions instead of making assumptions, Green."

"Christ, I really hope you're guilty of this."

"I got an idea. After I catch the guy who did this, let's you and me fight," I said.

I'd let myself get angry. I bet it showed.

"You're threatening an officer?"

"Don't you want to hit me?"

"Real bad I do, August."

"I'll sign a letter of immunity and let you try," I said.

"You said *catch the guy*, just now. Guy? Maybe it's the brunette."

"The guy I referenced wasn't gender specific. I intended it as a non-binary pronoun. Keep up, Green."

"Yeah, maybe I'll hit you after this. I'll visit you in prison." His phone rang. He looked at the screen and said, "Your time's up. I gotta go."

I stood. He stood.

"You're a nincompoop if you think I did this, Green."

"I follow facts, August."

His phone still rang. It was about me.

"You're following a false trail. So I'll solve it for you." I shot him with my finger and I left.

13

I spent the remainder of the day at my office researching Danil Turgenev and learning nothing new. I called the mysterious phone numbers again, but they remained disconnected or unhelpful. Tomorrow I was driving to Brooklyn and Newark and visiting the addresses found in his email. It was an easy seven hour drive. I'd spend the night and return the following day.

I messaged Jason Hicks' friends and his neighbor the dentist and finally connected with two of them, but they said nothing of substance. Nice guy, the *nicest* guy, who would ever kill a realtor. I called Jason's realty office and received the same story from the office manager, who grew weepy halfway through, and she said she would email me a list of current and recent clients. And no, the police hadn't asked for a similar list.

In my desk drawer, a bottle of Johnny Walker Blue sat on its side and today called for a dram. I drank straight from the bottle, which made a sucking pop when I lowered it. I reinserted the cork and paced the room. This was day four of the investigation into the innocence of

Mackenzie August, and I'd made satisfactory progress, but had I made enough? Was I racing against Roanoke City Police?

Tomorrow's trip to NYC could be revelatory, and I needed to hear from Marcus Morgan about the Russian mob. That was the key to this—Danil's former Russian connections.

Jason Hicks felt like a dead end.

I paced and I worked through my last few days, remembering early evidence through the lens of recent insight, and time passed and the traffic diminished and I realized I was late for dinner.

I drove home.

The coterie at Chez August was gathered in the kitchen, watching Manny cut grilled chicken thighs, and drinking spirits of their choice. Coldplay warbled softly from the speakers.

Noelle Beck was here too, perched on a stool at the counter, watching him, like a respectful student.

I thought Manny was in love with her. Except he didn't know what love was. No, that wasn't it. His love was too great a thing to focus on one person. No, still wrong. Maybe it was that love looked and felt different for him, or that he wouldn't let himself love her, not romantically, so he acted like a protective sibling. Or a mother hen.

Whatever it was, a lot of women would like to perch on a stool and watch Manny, close enough to touch, but that would never be tolerated by the man with the knife. Exceptions were consistently made, however, for Noelle Beck.

Kix sat in the corner, assembling toy cars into a line, too busy to say hello. Georgina Princess was happy to see me, at least. She walked over for a scratch and returned to the carpeted television area, laying down and forming a protective wall near Kix, between him and the door.

"Helga cleaned again," I said.

Stackhouse was drinking a beer and she set the bottle down with a thunk.

"Dammit. How's he know that?"

Manny sniffed. "*Cleaned.*"

"Helena," said Ronnie. "She cleaned yesterday. Or the day before."

"I must've been too tired to notice the disaster."

"What gave it away? The only difference is that our bathroom upstairs is cleaner."

"She mopped the floors with an adulterant."

"An adulterant? What do you normally use?" said Timothy.

"Water and pure castile soap. Obviously."

"Sometimes," said Manny, "I drop in lavender essential oil."

My father turned in a circle on the hardwood.

"Does it not look the same it always does?"

"This is what the floors in Chernobyl look like, old man," I said.

"I told the maid," said Manny, "about the streaks on the table."

"There were no streaks!" Stackhouse shouted.

"We call her a housekeeper," said Ronnie. "Not a maid."

"I told her, but she almost started crying, poor *criada*, and I told her forget it."

Stackhouse closed her eyes. "What is wrong with you two gorgeous men."

Noelle Beck was a woman finding out her parents sometimes fought and it alarmed her. She twisted on the stool to look at our wooden dining table. "I don't see streaks."

"*Por supuesto no*. I cleaned it when she left. You think I eat on a dirty table?"

"It wasn't dirty!"

"Here's why I don't like Helga," I said. "She shortcuts the work of being human."

"Oh Lord," said Stackhouse. "It's like sitting in church caught between dueling preachers."

"Why are we here?" I said. "Why are we alive? Does humanity exist to scroll Instagram reels? To watch television? We've dishonored the noble nature of work. Work is living, work is good. The divestiture of it leads to ruin. For example, the Roanoke City police detectives are shortcutting their work. They want the easy way, so they aren't being thorough, and they have the wrong guy. Forget it's me for a minute. Think of the disrespect paid to Jason Hicks' family with this shirking of duty. The detectives don't want to look for more fingerprints. They don't want to take more depositions. They don't want to investigate additional suspects, because it's exhausting. They have the wrong man, and justice is subverted. The right man, the real killer, isn't being considered, because they don't want to work, and it could lead to further destruction. In a more charitable mood, I'd say it's because the detectives have too many responsibilities, because they don't have the manpower, because we don't want to pay them more, because it would require more from the taxpayer, and God forbid work is asked of us. Streaks on the floor and the table matter, because they're an indication of shortcuts, of stunted growth, of subverted justice, of the easy way. Easy is cheap, easy corrodes your soul. Build yourself of metal, of hard work, of organic free range chicken, of honesty and sweat, and never use Pine Sol on my floors."

Manny raised his beer. "*Ay dios*, I'll read that manifesto every day, *amigo*."

My father pushed his glasses up and rubbed the corners of his eyes with this thumb and forefinger. "His mother used to be like that too."

"Now I feel bad about my eggs," said Beck.

"I'm too tired," said Stackhouse, "to refute that diatribe. I barely followed it."

Manny wiped his hands on the rag. "Dinner's ready in two minutes. The chicken was slaughtered on the plains of this great county after living a full life, wandering free, like Lewis and Clark and Jack Reacher, fine Americans."

Ronnie came to me and took my hand.

"My husband." She spoke for my ears only. "You are tense. I see it in your neck and shoulders."

"I am tense. The investigation moves slowly."

"What drink can I pour for you?"

"I'll have what you're having," I said.

"Champagne."

"I would rather die."

A hard knock at the door shattered our warm moment.

Timothy answered it.

Detective Green stood in the doorway. Detective Archie Hart behind him. Beyond them, a squad car with its lights off, two uniforms standing ready at the front bumper.

Green's lips were pressed together, a thin white line. He wore a RCPD black windbreaker. He took us in. Me, the federal marshal, the NSA analyst with the Glock on her hip, the respected elementary school principal, the feared defense attorney, and the sheriff. And the dog, a boxer watching him with suspicion.

Kix looked up from his cars.

This gentlemen uses too much hair product. Do not, I repeat, do not *invite him for supper.*

"August," he said.

"Green."

"Come on outside?"

"Why?" Stackhouse wore her sheriff khakis. She set down the bottle and walked forward to stand in front of me. "Tell me why, Detective."

"Tell us all why." Ronnie seemed to grow taller. "And Mackenzie isn't speaking a word to the police."

"August." He spoke over them. "You wanna come out? Or do this here?"

What he wanted to say was to keep my hands where he could see them, but he didn't.

"Do what?" Manny walked forward too, still wiping his hands with a dishrag. "Where he goes, we all go, *pendejo*."

Green swallowed. He was, I thought, doing better than most would be. The whole thing was hard and embarrassing.

"Fine," said Green. "Screw it, we'll do it here. You're under arrest, Mackenzie August. Two counts of murder in the first degree, Jason Hicks and Donald Torres. And you're under arrest for the abduction and manslaughter of Maddic Owens."

14

Like the rest of the world, I'd watched the televised attack on the Capitol Building, January 6th, 2021.

For a lot of reasons, it was an ill-advised attack.

The day of, the assault went surprisingly well. The intruders breached the Capitol and disrupted the formalization of the election. Congress was forced out. The halls emptied and the insurgents walked where they pleased. Mission accomplished, with only a few losses. Insurgents later stated they were stunned by their success. They flexed their muscles and made their case, a gratifying and triumphant day for them.

Trouble was, it was a short-term, pyrrhic triumph. Their victory, won by a surprise attack, rattled the world, especially law enforcement. The overwhelming might of Mother Justice roused and devoured them, and the insurgents could only plea and apologize in defense. They'd made their case but the Constitution remained unmoved.

I'd done something similar in Los Angeles, fifteen years ago. I was a uniformed officer working with Violent

Crimes, and I took exception with a guy in Vice. Guy named Gonzales, a corporal, an alcoholic ass that everyone hated, and I was an over-caffeinated rage monster on steroids, and I picked a fight with him in the parking lot. He'd been there with four Vice guys but I didn't care. I told Gonzales I was going to hit him and he dared me and I did. I sent him to the hospital, a gratifying triumph. However, the other four guys took exception. One of them had been Manny, already plainclothes with Vice for months. They beat me purple, until Manny called them off, and left me on the cold blacktop. Later, our Sergeants demanded explanations, why I was half-dead and Gonzales was in the ER with a concussion and broken orbital bones. No one told. Though I dodged severe reprimand, it set my career back months, because my judgment had been awful and everyone knew it. I made my case at the wrong time.

What I should have done was knock on his door later. Just me and him.

~

IN MY DOORWAY NOW, Green and Hart hadn't drawn their sidearms.

Subduing them would be child's play. Manny could do it himself. Part of him wanted to, I knew, the wild animal within. The six of us in the house, looking at the two jokers in our doorway, two jokers with bad information, telling me, an innocent man, I had to go to a cage, we didn't have to let it happen. If I said so, I thought even Stackhouse would walk them back, potentially at the cost of her career.

Because Green had it wrong. We knew he had it

wrong. And we could do something about it right now, and it would feel good, a gratifying victory.

But the Constitution would be unimpressed.

So what I would do was knock on Green's door later, just me and him.

15

"Maddie Owens?" Stackhouse gaped like a fish. "She's *dead*?"

"The Roanoke socialite, Maddie Owens?" said Ronnie. "You think Mackenzie *abducted* her?"

The name came back to me. Maddie's husband, Dr. Everett Owens, had been accused of burgling his neighbors and he lost his job at the hospital. He hired me to prove his innocence. I had, laying the blame at the feet of his wife, Maddie, and his neighbor Randal Dawson. Maddie had been humiliated, and I hadn't heard from her since.

"August, you coming outside?" said Detective Green.

"You sonofabitches," said my darling wife. "It's Friday night."

My father's skin was pale. "Does that matter?"

"It means I can't arrange for Mackenzie's bail until Monday, at the earliest. Or maybe Wednesday, depending on the judge's rotation. Detective Green did this on purpose."

Archie Hart held up his hands like shields. “No, no, ma’am. It’s not like that. We found new evidence today.”

“We gonna let them do this, *amigo*?” said Manny.

“Yeah. We are,” I said.

“Oh my God.” Timothy held onto the couch for support. Noelle Beck took his right arm.

“Maddie Owens is dead? Why wasn’t I told?” said Stackhouse.

“Found her today, ma’am.” Archie ducked his head, like apologizing for it. “Along with additional incriminations.”

Crimson was rising high into Ronnie’s cheeks.

“What evidence?” said Ronnie.

“You don’t want to do this here.” Green gave his face a little shake, watching her. “Trust me. You’re an attorney. File a got’damn motion for discovery and read the reports yourself, now he’s charged. Not here.”

“Mackenzie, you don’t say a word other than invoking your right to remain silent, and your right to an attorney,” said Ronnie. “You have to say it. I can’t say it for you.”

The world was moving for me in dream-like lurches.

“They are so invoked,” I said.

“Did you hear that, detectives? We did,” said Ronnie.

“We heard. Roger that.” Hart was still ducking his head.

“August.” Green held out his hand. “Let’s go.”

Stackhouse threw up her hands. Disgusted.

“Get my coat, babe, and I’ll drive.”

Ronnie nodded. “Yes.”

“That’s not necessary, ladies,” said Green.

“Is it not my got’damned jail? Am I not the got’damned sheriff?” said Stackhouse.

“Listen, okay, how about I make it easy. August has

already invoked his rights, so we won't question him. Not until Monday morning at nine. We heard that, right Archie? No need for you girls to be there. You want, you can watch him be processed—"

"We do want," said the sheriff.

"Call them girls again," said Manny, "and maybe you leave here without your ass."

I set my wallet and phone and keys onto the table. The noises sounded too loud. I was still resisting the impulse to preserve my freedom with violence.

Later. Later.

No short-term victory.

What new incriminations had been discovered? Whoever was framing me, he was a pro.

I walked outside and surrendered myself into police custody.

The uniformed guys wouldn't look at me. They wouldn't look at anything. Their uniforms were dark blue, buttoned up to the neck.

I stood facing the cruiser and Archie frisked me. He had to, it was the law.

Green Mirandized me.

Archie cuffed my hands behind my back. He didn't clamp them tight, and I made a note to buy him a drink next time I was on the outside, after I finished hitting him.

Stackhouse didn't take the driver's seat—Manny did. Ronnie in the passenger, Stackhouse in the back. They waited with doors open, watching us.

Neighbors watched from windows, backlit silhouettes.

A lesser man would've been mortified.

"You know what's sad, Green?" I said.

"This whole thing is sad, August."

"What's sad is, I have a better chance of cracking your case from jail than you do from within your freedom."

He opened the door and I ducked in and sat in the back. The stinking cold vinyl. The door slammed and I was sealed inside. Freedom revoked.

16

I prided myself on being something of a stoic. Prepared for anything, unswayed by emotion. Focused on what I could control. My happiness depended little on external things. That kind of stuff.

Being transported as a prisoner to jail, where I'd spend at least two nights, maybe four, maybe a lot longer, was taking a toll on my happiness.

Seneca would be disappointed.

The cops weren't talking and Campbell Avenue was deserted. Their radio squawked once and the driver turned it down, and I was jostled in my cage.

The cruiser turned into the alley beside the jail and waited for the rear garage door to rattle upward into the ceiling. The cruiser eased forward and the door trundled down behind us and locked. The cops, dressed in black, got out, and two deputy sheriffs spoke to them while I sat in the back seat. The deputies wore brown slacks and darker brown shirts, a golden sheriff's emblem on their shoulder, and a badge over their right breast. Their names were embroidered above their pocket. There was no joking or laughter in evidence. The cop opened my door and told me to step out and to sit on the dirty wooden bench, and I did. The garage was chilly and I wished I'd brought a jacket. I waited for twenty minutes, hands behind my back, the two Roanoke City police officers vigilant against my escape, and deputies filling out papers to assume responsibility.

I felt the annoying need to apologize to them.

Detectives Green and Hart appeared at the interior door and signaled for me. I didn't know the two sheriff deputies but they must've known me, because I wasn't yanked to my feet. Instead they nodded at me. A show of respect. I stood and walked to the detectives Green and Hart, bracketed by the sheriff deputies, and the two uniformed RCPD officers returned to their cruiser, their job done. Custody had been transferred.

Green led the way down a stark white hallway to the Magistrate, a civil officer behind a glass window. He was bald and Black, and he wore reading glasses and the expression of a man wishing he spent his Friday nights elsewhere.

Green testified under oath a list of complaints against me and the Magistrate listened through the hole in the glass, typing into a computer. I was still poleaxed by the Maddie Owens charge—abduction and manslaughter. While Green spoke, Stackhouse, Ronnie, and Manny arrived inside the hallway and listened. This interested the Magistrate more than I did. Each of them had a right to be here—the sheriff, my defense attorney, and a federal marshal—but still, the sight was unusual. The Magistrate sat up straighter and declared there was probable cause to arrest me and that I would be held without bond. He looked at the sheriff to see if he was doing the right thing, but this point in the judicial process was mere pageantry; an official checklist told him I had to be held without bond, and his job was merely to pronounce it.

Judgment rendered, Green took me by the arm and led our procession to intake. A large room with tables and drunks and deputy sheriffs standing around watching television. The atmosphere was relaxed, and Archie Hart released my handcuffs.

I knew this area; I'd been inside intake before, voluntarily, as a guest.

Stackhouse was talking on her cellphone. Manny was glaring at the detectives and they were pretending he wasn't.

I took Ronnie's face into my hands and kissed her.

"Think of it," I said, "like I'm going on vacation. All-inclusive."

"I spoke to the Commonwealth's Attorney on the way over. He recused himself and assigned a special prosecutor from Montgomery County. I left a message. The clerk's office opens at 8am on Monday, and I promise, Mackenzie, I'll get you out the first second I can."

"My faith in you reaches to the moon."

"That's it?" She tried to smile. "Mine touches the stars."

I knew she had to be wondering about the Maddie accusation. Maddie Owens was a lively sexpot, the sum of good-breeding and money and plastic surgery and sin, and she'd made multiple passes at me in front of Ronnie. I hadn't seen her in two years. Ronnie's faith in me might reach the stars, but how much evidence could be accumulated before that faith wobbled?

"Go home," I said. "Focus your energy on being a mom."

"You're fine," she said.

"I am fine."

"I know. You always are, Mackenzie. I'm telling it to myself. You're fine."

"I'll come see you tomorrow, *amigo*," said Manny. "See if you need anything."

"I'd rather you mow the grass."

"I don't garden," he said.

"Water the peonies, please."

"Ay, I'll join you in prison first."

Stackhouse finished her phone call and spoke softly to each deputy, men she knew by name because she'd hired them, and each was pale and sweaty when she was finished.

Manny took Ronnie by the hand and led her out. Stackhouse kissed me and she left too. The heavy metal door slammed and locked, disturbing the sleep of a drunk at the table.

Mackenzie August. Ward of the State.

I was provided an orange jumpsuit and told to change in the bathroom. I did, and I placed my clothes into a plastic bin. The bin was taken from me. Green walked me to the photo booth. My photograph was taken, my information recorded, and I was booked.

Archie ducked his head, still apologizing.

"Alright, Mack. Sit tight. If you didn't do this, justice will prevail. Soon as it can."

"It is not me you should be worrying about, Archie. I met your cousin, by the way. Imani. Nice girl."

"How'd you meet her?" he said.

"I was investigating. You should try it."

Green grabbed Archie by the shoulder and said, "Let's go home, Arch. To our nice warm beds and let the inmate go to his. Good luck, August, and hold onto that soap, huh."

They left too, the door booming again.

A deputy selected a mattress pad and stack of linens from the closet and laid the load into my arms. He said, "Not sure you'll fit on the bed, big guy." He led me down a hall with one-way mirrors looking into holding cells, up the stairs to the third floor, and through a portal that locked on both ends.

As we walked, he told me the rules.

Keep my cell clean, my bed made, personal effects neat and orderly. Keep the floor spotless, do not damage or deface walls or the ceiling. Do not touch a fellow inmate's belongings. Do not approach a deputy sheriff. No contraband.

A loud buzzer sounded inside the portal and the far iron door opened.

I'd never been this far inside the jail, but I knew the jail was divided into pods. Twenty cells per pod, with a central gathering area. Prisoners weren't sealed into their cells; they could mingle inside the pod.

I was surprised to see the pod's concrete walls were pale orange. The flecked tile floor was painted an aquamarine blue, like we swam in a coral reef. No windows. Two guys wearing jumpsuits played cards at a table in the central area, and they didn't seem interested in me. I was walked to cell nine, on the main level. There was a second level above mine, a walkway with ten more cells. Five of the cells we passed were occupied by guys on their beds. It was late and they were tired from the exhausting nothing that happened all day.

"Home sweet home," said the deputy.

I had a bench and a bed, a stainless steel sink and toilet. That was all. The lights inside my cell were off.

My cell.

This was where America deemed I be kept for the safety of her citizenry.

Jiminy Christmas.

17

Only the dining room light burned. Ronnie and Stackhouse and Timothy and Manny sat around the table, their faces light and shadow.

Timothy felt numb.

He said, "I don't understand. Could you explain it to me, as though talking to an ignorant old man?"

"Yes." Ronnie nodded. She took a deep breath, and let it out. Another one. Then, "Starting at the beginning. Evidence was found incriminating Mackenzie in two homicides, but it wasn't enough to indict him. We knew that much—the DNA under their fingernails, and Mackenzie's lack of strong alibis. The detectives continued their investigation until today, when additional evidence was discovered, enough for the detectives to take a bill of indictment to the grand jury, a group of local Roanoke citizens who examines evidence related to serious crimes. The grand jury considered the findings and issued a true bill, or warrant for Mackenzie's arrest. Detective Green called the Commonwealth's Attorney to alert him, but the CA knows me and Mackenzie, which means he can't be impartial, so he stepped out of the case and appointed a special prosecutor from Christiansburg who doesn't know us. The same process will probably occur with the judge, because I know them all. Mackenzie was arrested, and normally he would be questioned immediately, the detectives hoping to induce a confession before he asked for an attorney or invoked his right to silence, but I quashed that. Instead, they'll question him Monday, with me present, and they'll get nothing. I will file a motion for discovery, meaning get access to the evidence, which they've wisely kept hidden until now. I already left a message for the prosecutor, arranging a bond hearing, where I will argue that Mackenzie should be released on bail, and the judge will make a determination. I think I can get him out, but it's not a black-and-white thing. I'll do everything I can, including suggesting an ankle monitor, because Mackenzie's best chance might be to catch the true perpetrator himself. He's good at that, we all know. The special prosecutor will begin meeting with the detectives and reviewing the evidence, building a case against Mackenzie. I will begin discovery, and filing a mountain of fucking motions. The prosecutor and I will set a trial date."

"Do you predict this will go to trial?" said Timothy.

"Detectives and prosecutors don't like to lose. They must consider the new evidence dispositive."

"Which means?"

"Whatever it is with Maddie Owens, it was damaging," said Ronnie.

"How? There's absolutely no way Mackenzie abducted and murdered a woman," said Timothy.

"Not murder. Manslaughter." Stackhouse was leaning backward in her chair, her eyes closed. "Means Maddie's death was unintentional."

"That's significant, because the other charges were murder in the first degree. This is different. I'll know more Monday. We'll set a trial date, but I'll destroy this whole city to prevent one. You never know what a jury will do."

Manny was reclining on the couch, eyes far off, and he was pulling thoughtfully on his lower lip.

"If it looks bad, me and Mack running off to Argentina. We been threatening to for years."

"Not without me, you won't," said Ronnie.

"Polly origami?"

"*Polygamy*, but I hope you'll bring Noelle."

"To Argentina?" Manny grinned. "With that pale skin, *Señorita* have cancer by Tuesday."

Mackenzie's phone rang and they jumped. It was midnight. Ronnie picked the iPhone up with fingers that trembled.

"According to the ID," she said, "Marcus Morgan is calling."

"Want me to answer?" said Manny.

"No. I will."

"Remind me who Marcus Morgan is," asked Timothy.

"Local cocaine *jefe*."

"Good lord."

"*Ay dios*." Manny shot the sheriff a look. "I meant, local realtor."

Stackhouse didn't open her eyes.

"I know him and I know what he does."

Ronnie answered the call.

"Hello Marcus. It's Ronnie." A pause. "He isn't here. The dumbass fucking cops arrested him." Pause. "I know why Mackenzie came to see you. Tell me and I'll relate it to him Monday morning. Please."

Ronnie listened, but not long. The message was short.

"Thank you, Marcus." Pause. "You too. My love to Courtney."

She hung up.

"Mackenzie asked Marcus to look into the death of Donald Torres. Mackenzie suspects Russian mob ties. Marcus asked around, but came up with nothing. The local crew knows nothing about him. It's another dead end."

"*Maldición.*"

"What," said Timothy August, "in the hell is going on with my son."

18

I was awake the next morning when the lights buzzed on. It was early. Early-to-rise meant earlier-to-bed, and fewer problems at night for prison wardens. The buzzer rang loudly, a warning, and the cell doors unlocked.

This jail housed short-term guests. Intended for incarcerations shorter than a year, or persons waiting on hearings or trials or sentencing. It was kiddie jail. The big bad dudes were locked up in state or federal penitentiaries for decades. If my charges were brought to trial, and if I lost, I would be remanded to custody until sentencing, and I'd be here three more months while my transfer was processed to a long-term facility, like Big Stone Gap.

I had not slept well. And I thought I could be forgiven for it.

Deputy Cobb performed a roll call and stopped at my cell with a clipboard. Introduced himself—big guy, lifted weights, had all his dark hair—and read me the rules again, along with feeding times.

"Any questions?"

"What about coffee," I said.

"Coming soon. But it tastes like shit."

"Is it hot and wet?" I said.

"Tastes like warm and wet shit."

"Unacceptable. Ring for the concierge, please."

He grinned. "Concierge." He walked back the way he came.

Five minutes later I was considering the ceiling and another face popped at my door. Wiry guy with blue tattoos up to his chin, couldn't weigh more than Ronnie, though taller. His skin was pocked with meth mites from adolescence.

"You know, thought I heard Cobb said Mackenzie August, but I couldn't believe my ears, so I had to see it with my own eyes. Hot damn, if it isn't the big man himself," he said.

The guy in my doorway was named Hot Damn. That's how I knew him, because that's what everyone called him, including himself. He'd even asked an assistant Commonwealth's Attorney to call him that during a deposition. Hot Damn had been a witness to two violent crimes I'd investigated. I'd taken his testimony on both occasions, and prepped him for cross-examination, and we got on.

"Hot Damn," I said. "You look different without all the jewelry."

"Ain't that some bull." Hot Damn touched his ears and his nose, once adorned with gold rings, now plain. "They made me take'm off. I don't know what they thought I would do with them, dig my way out, maybe. They said they'd give me plastic shit to keep the holes from closing, but I ain't walking around with plastic in my face."

"I can't imagine the ignominy."

"The what?" he said.

"I can't imagine the public embarrassment."

"Yeah, that's right, you talk weird."

"I speak with the tongues of angels, Hot Damn," I said.

"Whatever. Why're you in here?"

"I killed three people."

"You did not."

"I did not," I said. "But don't tell anyone. The truth will ruin my street cred."

"You got lucky, did you know that? It's squeeze dog day."

"Squeeze dog," I said. "Unpack that for me."

"Unpack huh?"

"What is a squeeze dog?"

"Broiled hotdogs wrapped in white bread, for lunch. Best day of the whole damn week, August."

"Fortune smiles. Why're you in here, Hot Damn?"

"Some bull where I broke this guy's nose with a shovel, but he shouldn't'a been there anyway. My third strike."

"That was your fifteenth strike," I said. "At minimum."

"Yeah." He grinned the grin of a man who never invested in dental care. "Yeah maybe I lost track. I just can't believe Mack August is in here with me. C'mon, it's feeding time and you gotta meet the animals."

We formed a line at the bars and deputy Cobb slid us trays of food. Weak orange juice, burnt coffee, watery eggs, toast, two pats of butter, and a fruit mixture, mostly grapes and cherries.

Prison was a thousand small humiliations, like waiting in line for bad food.

Why the hell was I in prison.

I joined the herd with my tray.

Hot Damn stood over me like I was his property. Twelve other guys sat at the long picnic-style table. He addressed the animals.

"Listen up." No one did, but be bravely carried on. He was, I thought, the runt. "This's Mack August. Outside he's a private cop. Not a real one, a private guy. He saved my ass a couple times on bullshit I didn't do. He's with us. He's under my protection."

No one cared.

Hot Damn sat across from me. "There. You're good now, brother."

"Whew," I said.

I tried the eggs...

Nope. Not yet. I'd have to get a lot hungrier.

I drank the juice and dropped the two pats of butter into my coffee and stirred it, and found the concoction improved enough to enjoy. I ate the grapes too.

"You put butter in your coffee. Hot damn, August, you're built different, ain't you."

"Like creamer. Try it."

"I need butter for the bread," he said.

"Skip the bread."

Guy next to Hot Damn, a Black guy with the beginnings of an afro, who wore his orange jumpsuit with the arms tied around his waist, snorted at me.

"Be here a few weeks, man, you eat the bread. Bread ain't bad. Can't mess up the bread, man, you know what I'm saying. Bread's the thing this fucking zoo can't mess up."

I raised my plastic mug of coffee to him.

"I defer to the expert."

"If you ain't gonna eat it." The guy reached across and took it. "I'll use it for hooch."

"You're brewing?"

"Got a bottle of cherry and one strawberry. Need the

bread for yeast. Got another empty bottle, got the juice boxes, but not enough sugar yet."

The twelve other inmates—eight were White, three Black, one Latino. These weren't bad dudes. More like idiots, instead of hardened careers. These guys had arrived to jail malnourished, and they smoked cigarettes and joints instead of eating, and spent money on tattoos instead of child support. I was stereotyping them into a monolithic inmate, but I was close. They looked sullen and pale, and I listened to them talk to each other like mountebanks. There was one exception, the gentleman at the end, a bald-headed White guy, taller than me, heavier than me. He looked maybe fifty, scruff on his chin and around his ears going white. Some of the guys ate eggs until their stomachs refused more, and they set their trays in front of him, and he ate the eggs.

"That's Mr. Clean," said Hot Damn.

"The big guy."

"Don't got no hair. Quiet dude. Likes to sweep. Mr. Clean. He the best fighter."

"Fighter?" I said.

"Hell yeah. Guys here, we get bored. Of course we're bored. And we love to fight. It ain't like a prison riot, and we ain't mad. It's a sport. Look'it." Hot Damn pointed at a guy three seats down. The guy's eye was swollen shut, and his lip was purple. "No one jumped him. He fought Dirty Jake. Dumbass thing to do, but he wanted it. Pigs let it go on a few minutes before they break it up. I gotta fight Mr. Clean next."

"You have to?"

"Kinda."

"The giant has a hundred pounds on you," I said.

"It's my turn."

"You told me it's like a sport."

"It is."

"If you have to, it's not volitional. It's not a sport," I said.

"It's not what?"

"Sports are voluntary."

"Oh. I mean," he said. "I ain't being forced to. It's not like that."

"What's it like?"

"I volunteered."

"You volunteered to get your head kicked in," I said.

"You want to be one of the guys, you fight." Hot Damn shrugged. "It's simple."

"Fight someone littler."

"I did! I won. Four weeks ago. It's my turn again, and it's Mr. Clean's turn."

"Your chances of winning," I said, "are not ideal."

"He takes it easy on me. I don't have to beat him to win! We ain't insane! I gotta stay awake for two minutes, is all. If I quit, I lose."

The guy next to Hot Damn, the guy with the afro, said, "Better lose than quit."

"I ain't quitting," said Hot Damn. "Hell no I ain't quitting."

Honor among thieves, and pride among convicts.

"You a private cop?" said Afro. "Money in that?"

"If one's industrious."

"Huh?" he said.

"If you work hard. What'd you do before this? Make moonshine in the hills?"

"Nah. I moved shit."

"For who?" I said.

"Brother named Edgar. I moved shit for Edgar."

"Edgar, owns the gun stores?" I said.

He grinned. Two missing teeth, three gold teeth, one silver.

"You know my man Edgar."

"He knows me. Sometimes we run in the same circles, but opposite directions. He hosts a card game I've played in," I said.

"Oh shit. You play that game?"

"Used to. That's not my world. Fat Susie died working for us, and somehow the mafioso lost its shine."

"You knew Fat Susie," he said.

"We loaned him out from Big Will and Marcus."

The guy leaned back and hit Hot Damn in the shoulder.

"Big Will!" The guy made a hooting noise. "Shoot, this boy's major. He ain't under your protection, Hot Damn. His ass don't need protection. We need protection from him!"

"What'd I tell you." Hot Damn looked a little diminished. If I didn't need a protector and prison guide, he was less important."I tole you he's with us."

"He ain't with you, Hot Damn. He's your damn boss, boy, what he is, hanging out with Big Will and Edgar."

"My boss, shit. I don't know those guys," said Hot Damn.

"Cause you White. Cause your ass doing meth, what it's doing. Big Will ain't your boss, this guy is."

"August," said Hot Damn. "What's he talking about? You ain't a boss, right?"

"I'm on my own. When I meet with Big Will and Edgar, it's to tell them to stop doing something," I said.

"You told Big Will to stop shit?" said Afro.

"I have."

"What'd he say?"

"He was resistant," I said. "But we worked it out."

"You and Big Will worked it out. Got'damn, I don't get this."

From down the table, a guy with red hair yelled at me. He couldn't have been more than nineteen.

"Yo Mr. August, you remember me?"

I did, vaguely. But couldn't place him. I told him so.

He said, "You taught my English class at Patrick Henry."

"Ah hah. That's it. You were good with Shakespeare."

He broke into a big red grin. "That's right. I was."

"Your name's Kyle," I said.

"That's right!. You remember."

"Looks like I failed you, Kyle. If I'd taught you better, you'd be the governor by now, instead of in prison."

He still grinned. "No, you was the best teacher I ever had. This is my own fault."

"When you get out, look me up. We'll talk about the rest of your life."

"Oh yeah?" He grinned down at his tray instead of at me.

Afro across from me said, "You taught him? You teach?"

"Not anymore."

"Now you deal with Big Will and Edgar. What the hell do you do for money? I mean, exactly?" he said.

"I work privately for clients, doing what cops don't want to do," I said.

"Can I do that?"

Half the table was listening to us now.

Mackenzie August, show stealer.

"Not if you're a felon," I said.

"What if my lawyer makes that shit go away?" he said. "You make money? I get out, I'm gonna make real money and help the world, you know?"

"First put your home in order."

He looked at me half a minute. The whites of his eyes were a little yellow.

"My home? The hell's that mean?"

"You asked if you can do what I do. Maybe. First step, put your home in order."

"I don't get that."

"To put your home in order, first discipline yourself," I said.

"That's like a poem or something? Some shit somebody said about something?"

"It's a maxim but I'm botching it."

"Discipline myself? I still don't get that," he said.

"Learn self-control. Go to bed early, get up early, even when nobody's making you. Eat well. Control yourself. Start making money. When your life is ordered, help order the lives of those you live with. Then help order your street. Then neighborhood, then the city, and you are changing the world."

"Man." He shook his head like he'd gotten angry at a math problem. "Order my life? I don't get what you're talking about. I want to do what you do, that's all."

"What do you want him to do, Ray?" said Hot Damn. "Teach you how to be a man over breakfast? What's he gonna say? How's he gonna do all that? There ain't enough words!"

"Go to bed early? How come? How early?" said Ray, guy with the afro.

"Mastering yourself is hard. And those who can't have no business interfering in the world."

"Yeah but how come?" he said.

Hot Damn was right. There weren't enough words.

I said, "Gotta start somewhere. Start with bedtime."

"Yeah but why there?"

"Ray, with the questions. Jeez. When you get out, Ray, look me up. We'll talk it through."

Maybe I could go into business counseling ex-cons for no money. A niche market.

"Maybe I will," he said.

"But only if you stay away from Edgar and Big Will."

"Man, c'mon, how'm I gonna go that? That's my boss, you know what I'm saying."

"Not anymore. Because you'll be going to bed early," I said.

"But why?"

"Ray!" shouted Hot Damn. "Shut the hell up! Or I swear I'm going to freak out!"

It was, I thought, a fair point.

19

Manny brought me a book. *The Unsettling of America*, by Wendell Berry. I'd made it a third of the way through and I was already searching for plots of land to plow and plant crops and raise cattle, and save America through my earthy wholesomeness.

Perhaps Ray should read it.

Marshals like Manny had wide autonomy within the jail. Distilled down to its simplest form, their job was dealing with prisons. And Manny being Manny, he was revered and feared within. He walked up to the bars of our pod and handed me the book and Deputy Cobb only watched.

"I was a kid, I was in jail a couple times," said Manny.

"It's way worse now. We don't get HGTV."

"In Puerto Rico, they throw kids in with the monsters."

"In Roanoke, they eat the kids."

"In Puerto Rico," he said, "the warden beat us with hoses for using the toilet."

"In Roanoke," I said, "we don't have toilets. We hold it for weeks."

"In Puerto Rico, all the beds have bugs and *piojos*."

"In America, we have White guilt. Even the Black guys do," I said.

"*Ay caramba*. That's bad."

"You wouldn't survive a day in here. There's no hair gel."

"It's paste, not gel, *tonto*."

He and I were being watched. By everyone.

Manny crossed his arms and leaned against the bars, and he talked softly.

"*Tu amigo* Marcus says Donald Torres wasn't part of local mob groups. Or if he was, nobody told him. I talked to some people too. Nobody knew Torres or Turgev-whatever."

I nodded to myself.

Rats.

I'd been expecting clues from the underworld.

"Ay," Manny said. "You want out, you give me the signal. We be in Mexico tomorrow and drinking mescal in Argentina the day after."

Ah friendship.

Manny meant it. One of the things that made Manny Manny was his unwavering violent loyalty. He couldn't legally sign me out of jail, but he could manage it illegally. We would flee the country and he wouldn't think twice. In fact, I knew part of him thought it'd be an adventure, a chance to test himself, starting over in Argentina. He'd already planned it in his mind. Given the choice, he'd rather die helping a friend than die an old man without one.

"Let's wait," I said. And I was NOT close to tears. "We'll do this in a way that keeps your pension intact."

"Maybe I show you pictures of Argentinian women,

before deciding."

"They're not worthy of holding Ronnie's bikini," I said.

"The women would be for me, *amigo*."

"Ah."

"And I am a humble spic, and don't know how pension works anyway," he said.

"We don't say spic anymore."

"Prison gonna be good for you, toughen you up. All of soft America should spend time in here, give them real things to worry about, instead of scary words."

"Water my flowers," I said.

"Death first."

He left and I returned to my cell with my book.

It was reassuring to know I had an escape hatch. Which we absolutely wouldn't use.

Which we probably absolutely wouldn't use.

~

I READ for an hour before giving up. Not even Wendell Berry's impassioned, powerful, and precise prose could distract me.

Maddie Owens was dead. And somehow I was implicated.

Never before had I faced such a maddening challenge. Most guys went to prison, they knew why. They knew exactly why. In the case of Maddie Owens, I had no idea why. And I wouldn't know until Monday morning. Had Maddie still lived in Roanoke? Had she known Jason Hicks or Donald Torres? How had she died? Manslaughter meant they didn't think I killed her with a hammer, so that was nice. But I was still to blame. How could I be framed for accidentally killing her?

Whoever was doing this, they were excellent. I kept telling myself that, because it kept being obvious. But why did a pro want me dead?

There was no money in my death. Marcus would've told me if there was a contract out.

Why else would a pro be after me? Revenge.

...

That was all I could think of. Money or revenge, and revenge far more likely.

But then why not kill me, instead of framing me? Framing me took a lot more work.

Because they couldn't.

Why not?

Because they couldn't physically. Or they worried about Manny. Or they worried about repercussions from someone else, maybe Marcus.

If Ronnie's ex-fiancé was still alive, he'd be the primary suspect. But he wasn't.

I'd been through this before. Once an hour I went through these machinations.

Maddie Owens' death made it more complex, because I had direct connections to her. I'd ruined Maddie's life. She'd been forced to confess to an absurd string of crimes, ruining her social status as a debutante. Maddie Owens was a person who might want revenge against me. But she was no pro. Nor was anyone I could think of, outside the mafioso.

Which made Marcus' message disheartening.

And another thing! At my house last night, one of Green's statements caught my ear and worried me now.

Ronnie had demanded to know what evidence they had implicating me in Maddie Owens' death. Green had replied, *You don't want to do this here. Trust me.*

Trust me.

The implications were ugly for a wife being told her husband had abducted a woman.

After further considering the ceiling, I stood from bed and began jumping jacks. Then did up-downs, a football exercise. Maybe a good workout would clear my mind and calm my anxiety. I stripped off the orange jumpsuit. Back to jumping jacks, then more up-downs, which was a way coaches tortured their players. I switched to pushups, then back to up-downs, and took a break to breathe, and I did the whole thing over again.

Thirty minutes passed, and I was soaked with sweat.

I didn't feel any better, and nothing new occurred to me, but at least now I was gross too.

THERE WAS an audible buzz among the inmates at chow time. Squeeze dogs!

I stood last in line. When my turn came, Deputy Cobb slid me a tray. Two burnt hot dogs, each wrapped in a piece of bread. Sliced potatoes. A pale mush that looked like old corn. Four bites of watermelon. One packet of ketchup and one packet of mustard, and a container of milk.

I accepted the tray but Cobb didn't let go.

"August," he said. "We're moving you this afternoon."

"Where?"

"Out of general population. Orders came from the tippy-top."

"Sheriff Stackhouse," I said.

"That's what I was told."

"Tell her I said no thanks."

"No thanks?" he said.

"I'll stay here."

"Why?"

"It's lovely," I said.

"That won't fly. You're trying to get me fired?"

"Tell Stackhouse she'll have to personally mace me to get me out, and if she does then I'll never cook for her again," I said.

He looked a little dizzy.

"August, there ain't no way I'm telling her that. She's the sheriff. You get that? She's my boss's boss's boss."

"And she's got great cans?" I said.

"Good lord, August."

"You guys talk about it, I know you do."

"That doesn't mean—"

"You should see her in her pajamas," I said. "But you're being a little sexist, Cobb. I hope you don't call them cans. What descriptive word do you use?"

Behind Cobb, another deputy at the far end of the portal was grinning. I called to him. "How do you guys talk about the sheriff? What words are used?"

"No sir, I'm not telling you shit, sir, I believe I'll keep my job, thanks," said the guy.

"August." Cobb cleared his throat. "You're refusing to leave your pod?"

"Be a gentleman, Cobb. Ask her what term she'd prefer instead of cans. Tell I her told you to ask."

"August!" Cobb looked panicky. "Knock it off!"

"I'm telling her you called them cans."

"You're being a pain in my ass on purpose, but I'm only obeying orders, August. I'm not telling the sheriff, the got'damn *sheriff*, any of the things you told me to, because I'm getting married in two months and I need this job," he said and his voice cracked when he said married.

"Inform Stackhouse I'm not leaving until after the fight."

"What fight?" he said.

"I'm not telling you. You think I'm a snitch? It's us against you, Cobb, that's the first rule of being on the inside."

"I swear." Cobb wiped his mouth. "I swear I'm about to get fired."

He turned on his heel and walked back through the portal. The deputy grinning at me gave me a little salute and he left too, the far door closing with a clang.

Mackenzie August. Still not a grownup.

I sat in the same seat as breakfast. My fellow inmates were noisily eating.

Lord, I said to myself, *thank you for my health. Please do not let this meal destroy it. Please bless Ronnie and Kix today with peace and happiness. Amen.*

I tried a squeeze dog.

It's hard to mess up a hot dog, and thankfully they hadn't. Copious salt and pork and heat had been applied, and who could ask for more.

Hot Damn watched me for a reaction. His mouth was open and full of food, and he said, "It's good, right?"

"The banquet," I said, "is in the first bite."

"What?"

"I didn't know prison chow could be so good."

"See, it ain't that bad in here," said Hot Damn, but I saw his eyes flick down the table to Mr. Clean. The giant had three extra milks and two extra squeeze dogs in front of him.

Ill-gotten gains.

20

Friday night in prison had passed easily. I'd been protected by a cocoon of pride warmed by the thought of Detective Green's forthcoming humiliation. I would be vindicated and he would be on parking lot duty in hell. Or worse, Florida in July. Sleeping on a prison bunk had felt cute, or close to it, a once-in-a-lifetime experience, a kid at camp, not to be ruined by anxiety.

Tonight, Saturday, my release felt less assured. The walls solidified and encroached on my innocence. I lay within in a cavity of uncertainty, and the guy next door cried in his sleep.

The thing of it was, even after Ronnie secured my release, I wasn't sure what to do, other than knock at specific addresses in New York, which I had a sinking suspicion were dead ends. A diminishment of hope kept my eyes open.

I made a career out of entering relationships other people avoided, and chasing evidence through lions' dens. I caught Maddie Owens redhanded because I'd waded into her seedy world of sexcapades and adultery. I caught

Roland Wallace's would-be killer by walking into his small mansion and glaring at the suspects until the killer flinched. The hard, unpleasant work didn't faze me. I liked pressuring suspects, I like snuffling after vanishing threads.

But in my current investigation, I couldn't find them. No lions, no dens. There was a woman Jason Hicks danced with, who may or may not have been wearing a wig. That's *it*.

Donald Torres may or may not have been former Russian mafia. But I had no one to talk with about it. I had some addresses, which might bring me to doors opening into nothing, or they could open into the realm of the Russian *Bratzá*, and not even I, the world's foremost super sleuth, could pressure them. The absence of clues was alarming.

I *knew* this person. That aggravated me. Whoever was framing me, I knew him. And he knew me. Or her. Or them. No one meticulously framed a stranger.

Hopefully the death of Maddie Owens gave me more to go on, a ghastly sentiment. Otherwise, I might as well make myself at home.

...

Was I the world's foremost super sleuth?

I'd never heard of anyone better.

Then again, I was in prison. Not a ringing endorsement.

Private cops didn't attend conventions with awards. Like our profession, we were aloof and withdrawn, from what I'd seen. Happy, vulnerable persons would be pulverized by the work. In a room of private cops, the winner wouldn't accept the award. Because if he did, he'd be unworthy of it. Or her. Probably him, though, because women were lovely. And mine wasn't a career that suffered loveliness.

God and mother nature had conspired to make women lovely and desirable, to draw the male, and then make women nurturing, to raise young, and make men wielders of clubs to hit animals with and bring back steak.

I wouldn't want a woman—namely Ronnie—to have my job. Because I wouldn't want her to get hit.

Call me old fashioned.

But certainly old fashioned guys like me could be forgiven for thinking women were lovely and men should be the ones braving a lion's den. That of the two, men's bodies seemed better designed to dig and protect, and women's to nourish. Yet that simple observation of height and weight seemed out of vogue, likely to draw the ire of kids on Twitter.

I was an old-fashioned guy who'd married an empowered modern woman whose annual income lapped mine. What did I know.

My ideal further broke down when men used their clubs to hit each other, instead of dinner, filling up prisons. And when women were left without a man to protect their cave. Or when the woman didn't even want one to begin with. Hard to blame them, considering the guys I'd eaten dinner with.

On the other hand...

...on the other hand, Manny.

And Timothy August.

And Tom Hanks and Tim Tebow and Barak Obama and Dwight Eisenhower and Chris Hemsworth and John Legend. Men who stood at the doorway to their home—

I wondered what time it was. I'd fallen into fighting for

modern masculinity again, and hours could pass while I constructed airtight arguments against straw men.

Or straw women.

Whatever.

The simplest way to put it, being around Ronnie, tall and strong and soft and beautiful and feminine, made me want to be a man. A man whose strength came from character, from fidelity, from wisdom, courage, self-control, and passion. Who could argue with that notion?

Only maniacs who'd never seen Tim Tebow without a shirt, or heard John Legend sing.

Cause I give you aaalllll of me

And you give me aaaalllll of you.

Ronnie.

I felt Ronnie's absence like a physical thing. We should be together, and we weren't, and next to me lay a stranger uninvited. Instead of Veronica Summers, there was wickedness. Screwtape muttering accusations. Implying deficiencies. Telling me I should win arguments in my head, and that would fix things.

Ronnie's absence felt like fear and hate and insecurity.

I was a man convinced more happened in our world than what we could see, that evil had personality, and I was besieged by it.

I stood up and the bed creaked. The water at my sink was cold and I splashed it on my face, and I looked at the distorted man in the metal mirror. Afterward I leaned my head on the bars and I dripped from my chin.

"Mackenzie August," I said. "Too introspective for prison."

The prison bars were cold and unimpressed.

21

Sunday morning I went to chapel.

I sat on a hard metal folding chair in a room with a wooden crucifix, and the pale chaplain in a black cassock told me and twenty other prisoners that we should honor our father and mother, even when we didn't want to. That their behavior wasn't up to us, that we couldn't control them, but we could control ourselves, and we should honor them unconditionally, as befitted the Lord. We took communion afterward, and I returned to my pod feeling better, a spiritual being after all, one refreshed by the reminder of it.

Stackhouse waited for me at the portal to my pod, taller and more erect in her dominion, more beautiful by the comparison, and she took a handful of my jumpsuit and jerked me out of line.

"Prisoner abuse," I said.

"Mackenzie." She spoke through clenched teeth. "I'm doing my best here, babe, and you're not making it easy. Do you know how much better your father and your wife would sleep if they knew you were safe?"

"I'm perfectly safe."

"They don't know that. They think you're being raped continuously," she said.

"That's crass."

"All they know of prison, they learned from watching crass movies," she said.

"If anything, I would not be on the receiving end."

"Why won't you be transferred?"

"I like my pod," I said.

"Babe. You're pushing it."

We weren't alone, because we stood in a large hallway with deputies at the far end, and prisoners trying to eavesdrop on the other side of the bars, but with our voices low we could speak privately.

"I'm not leaving, because of Green."

"What about him?" she said.

"He put me in here and he's going to catch hell for it. But if I accept deferential treatment, then I won't earn it."

"Earn what?"

"The right to beat his ass when I get out," I said.

"You can't attack a detective."

"Can and will."

"No."

"I can't receive special treatment, because it'll hurt my claim to retribution," I said.

"You're an idiot."

"An honorable one."

"I won't tell Green I moved you," she said.

"It's not about him."

"Then..." Stackhouse looked defeated. "What's it about?"

"I need my own permission."

She rolled her eyes. "Oh God."

"I can't beat his ass unless it's warranted. But that's decided by me. By an inner arbiter. It's not the law of America; it's the law of Mackenzie. I'm not sure how else to explain it."

"It's pride."

"Pride's all I need," I said. "I am a hardened criminal now."

"I'm frustrated with you. And I might take it out on your father."

"Deputy Cobb deserves a raise," I said. "Make it happen."

"Deputy Cobb was told to transfer you and he didn't."

"That's my fault, not his. And I tried to get him to talk dirty about you but he wouldn't," I said.

"One of my deputies has some class?" She made a hmph noise and her eyebrows rose. Her eyebrows were a nice mixture of spa and spunk. "Good for him. Behind my back they usually call me Sheriff Brick House, or Sheriff Cans."

"Those insensitive bastards," I said. "But if they're behind your back, then they're looking at your ass. Shouldn't they refer—"

"Babe. Mackenzie. I'm something of a deviant. You can discuss my body all you want, and I'll enjoy it. But let's do it at your place, not in jail."

"A deviant with scruples," I said.

"Last chance. Do you want out of this pod?"

"No thank you. Home is where the heart is. Please tell Ronnie I'm healthy and in no danger."

"We'll get you out soon," she said.

"I know."

"If I kiss you, it'll be seen as preferential treatment."

"Better not. Reputation is everything in here."

I READ in my cell until I got bored.

To change things up, I read at the table.

Other guys played cards or watched the television or left for their jobs in the kitchen. A vent existed in the fourth cell, I was told, through which I could talk dirty with a woman housed on the second floor, for a price. I didn't inquire about the price. A basketball court was available to the inmates on the third floor, but I didn't want to be dunked on. The day felt mild, an apathetic glaze on the hours, and I wondered if Sundays were intentionally engineered to be days of rest.

The fight in our pod was scheduled for that evening, before lights out. Hot Damn drew further within himself every hour, and he sweated and refused food at chow time. As the anointed hour approached, so swelled the fervor. I remained at my table, listening to the chatter.

It wasn't a question of whether Hot Damn could beat Mr. Clean.

It was a question of time. How long before Hot Damn quit, or was rendered insensate? The prevailing opinion was, Hot Damn was wily and could stay on his bicycle (boxer lingo for running) long enough to reach two minutes. A bruising punchers' match would be more entertaining, but there was still value in tonight's exhibition.

I questioned Kyle further.

He said, no, Hot Damn didn't have to fight. But it was his turn and he'd been ducking it. If he refused, he'd essentially be an outcast, shunned by the group. Either he was one of them or he wasn't, and if he was then they took turns. Camaraderie and inclusion weren't things to be lightly tossed away, especially when you had nothing else.

And, he said, Mr. Clean didn't fight dirty and didn't break bones. Not always.

Time for the main event.

Men began lining the upper balcony. They sat at the rail, their legs dangling over, and they banged their hands on the bars. The long table and benches were bolted down, otherwise they would've been moved back, but as it was there was enough room. I still sat there, but I was the only one.

Cobb was gone for the day, and the nightshift deputies knew about the fight. They lingered by the portal bars to watch. If something went wrong, there was nowhere to run, and no one to help, because the guards were in on it.

Hot Damn squatted in his cell, three down from mine, throwing up. Mr. Clean was in his, the first cell, closest to the door. Waiting to be introduced.

Drama! Spectacle and pomp!

A guy I didn't know, a White guy, shifty looking, like he sold watches on the street, came to the middle of the pod and he was rubbing his hands together.

"Alright alright, let's get this bitch started, whaddaya think. Cause it's *that* time."

Hooting from the top rail. They shouted, *Ready to Rummmmble!*

I folded an ear down on the page—sorry, Mr. Berry—and closed my book.

The shifty White guy cracked some jokes about Mr. Clean's undefeated record, and Hot Damn's less than stellar record, and all the guys laughed about it. I didn't get the impression of hate or anger. It was more ritual than cruelty. You want in the pack? You play the game, even when it's not fun, and you get to sit and laugh on the rail next week.

Mr. Clean lumbered from his cell and the guys cheered. He wore his jumpsuit. I hadn't heard him speak in two days. Nor had he interacted with anyone beyond nods and shrugs. He stood next to the shifty guy, his hands in his pockets, kinda swaying back and forth.

It was Hot Damn's turn to make his appearance. In his cell, he was hopping up and down, working up some adrenaline and courage.

I stood.

"I'll play," I said.

The guys above didn't hear me over their clamor, but the shifty emcee did. He said, "Huh?"

"We take turns? It's my turn," I said.

"Damn, dude, you can fight next week."

"I'll fight now."

The spectators now shushed each other so they could listen.

"I'm fighting tonight." I said it louder for their benefit.

"It ain't your turn, it's Mr. Clean's turn."

"That's fine," I said.

"And it's sure as hell Hot Damn's turn."

"Me and Mr. Clean seem about even," I said.

Shifty started laughing like a man unsteady. "*Damn.* You *want* to fight Mr. Clean."

I nodded beyond him to the bald giant.

"This guy, he's a kitten," I said.

The deputies at the portal were talking to themselves. How far up their ass would Stackhouse's boot be if I died?

Shifty said, "Just cause you big don't *mean* you can fight Mr. *Clean*. Clean's undefeated."

"Consider it my initiation."

"I don't consider shit I don't wanna consider. Damn, it ain't your turn, new guy."

I unzipped my jumpsuit all the way down. I stepped out of it.

"I'm fighting," I said.

The crowd cheered, loudest they'd been yet. A plastic bottle of pinkish liquor was passed down the row, each man sipping under the watchful gaze of the rest.

Shifty said something to Mr. Clean that I didn't hear. In response, the giant shrugged and nodded. He unzipped his jumpsuit too, and Shifty threw up his hands in resignation.

Mr. Clean was thick with muscle.

Mackenzie August, thick with bad ideas.

"You can tap out, but you lose," Shifty shouted at me. "Or if you black out. Or if you die."

Hot Damn had lowered onto his bed, staring through the bars, both hands covering his mouth.

"Do me a favor," I said. "Stop him before I die."

"Damn, I was joking," said Shifty.

I pulled my T-shirt off too. I didn't want Mr. Clean to have much to grab. I stood before him in only boxers. He wore briefs and the T-shirt. He frowned at my uniform. Men on the rails mentioned the ludicrous KING tattoo across my back.

Wonder if I should explain to Mr. Clean that I'd won a bloodsport tournament in Naples, and they'd tattooed me without my consent.

Mr. Clean had no tattoos. But he had several inches and at least twenty-five pounds on me. Unless the smaller guy knew what he was doing, the bigger guy always won.

Sweat trickled down my chest and I felt a thrill of fear.

The fear was good. Made me alert, made me feel alive.

Mr. Clean made a motion, like—*come on*.

"*Damn*, I guess this shit's happening," said Shifty. I barely heard him above the howler monkeys. Another deputy arrived to watch.

I didn't mind losing. I'd lost fights before.

Wait. No.

I did mind losing.Very much. What I meant, losing wasn't the worst case scenario here. Getting my face ruined was. I'd rather not appear before the judge purple and swollen as my wife argued I was an upstanding citizen.

Shifty made a pumping motion with his fist and he ran to the stairs, and Mr. Clean and I were alone in the clearing.

I told Mr. Clean, "Tap out anytime," over the shrieking.

Mr. Clean came at me like a wrestler. He wanted to shoot at my knees, get his arms around me, take me down.

No sir.

I danced to my left. He got near and I snapped out jabs, peppering his unprotected face. Meaty smacks.

My knuckles stung, hitting his cheek and forehead, missing his nose.

August, you didn't even stretch! I was tight. A tight lunatic.

Kix. Don't be like your father.

Mr. Clean kept nearing, kinda crouched. I hit him a left jab, hard right cross, *smack smack*. I hit him good, but he caught me. We slammed against prison bars, cell five, and fell. I twisted like a maniac and slipped free, and his hands clawed gouges in my back.

Up again and dancing. His mouth bled and my left hand did too.

We did it again. He charged, I punched him hard enough to knock out smaller men, and we toppled over the table. I landed on my back, him on top, and my ribs cracked. He moved well for a big guy. I twisted to get loose but couldn't.

He was an elephant on my chest, me on my back, staring up, wondering what the hell.

Ground and pound, hitting me in the skull. I blocked and blocked and blocked, but he was sweaty and drooling now, hammering, hammering.

Not enough air.

Our spectators screamed.

Tap out?

Only two minutes in, I was pinned. I should accept the loss to preserve my face. But my pride. Toxic masculinity. Maybe the kids on Twitter were right.

But the bigger guy didn't know what he was doing.

The smaller guy did.

Mr. Clean bent over me too far and he paused to breathe, and I punched him in the throat. He made a, "Huuggk," and I hit him a combo in the nose. Three straight shots, left-right-left, awful. Cartilage crunched. He reeled, I thrust up with my hips, and he was dislodged and I scrambled to my feet. Put the table between us. My head rang and I sucked oxygen.

Behind me, Hot Damn was banging on his bars and shouting at me.

Being hit in the nose is the absolute worst. Mr. Clean's looked broken. Blood ran down his face, and the back of his throat. He couldn't breathe through his nostrils. Although he didn't know it, the fight had been decided.

It takes an animal to win a fight, and the animal inside him had retreated. He was mere flesh now.

"We're done," I told him. Despite the pain in my ribs, I was dancing. Fists held at my chin. "Tap out. Go lay down."

He didn't. He came on. Probably that's how'd he gotten through life without talking. He just kept coming, and coming, and it worked until you met someone like me.

I picked him apart like a sniper would. He got close, I hit him. Jabs and crosses he didn't know how to stop. He tried to charge, I hit and moved, he missed, gathered himself, shook his head, and tried once more, and I hit him more. Like a tank, he absorbed it, slowly breaking down.

His eyes swelled and puffed, and my hands hurt.

"This is stupid," I told him. "You gotta know when to stop."

He didn't.

I shouted at Shifty, "Make him stop."

"Damn, *you* make him stop!"

I felt sick, hitting him the nose and eyes more. I adjusted my aim to the joint of his jaw. I connected twice with my right, and eating tomorrow would be near impossible for him, but he remained upright.

"We're good!" I told him. "Go lay down."

He could barely see through the blood, through his inflamed brow and cheeks. He swayed unsteadily, always in my direction.

The thing was, Mr. Clean didn't know when to stop. He had bulk and strength and maybe nothing else, so this is what he did, and he couldn't stop. Even if it ruined him. His motor was a disability.

And me, an idiot with a club, hitting his neighbor, who couldn't hit back.

So I raised my hands, both bleeding, and waved them over my head.

"Okay." I was blowing air and sweating and my ribs complained. I thought they were broken. "I give. I'm done."

"What?" said Shifty. "*Damn*! You tap?"

What!

I pointed at Mr. Clean. "There's your winner. He outlasted me. My hands can't take anymore."

The crowd groaned as one. Colossal disappointment. They wanted to see a man unconscious.

Mr. Clean toppled forward and I caught him at forty-five degrees, and the pain in my chest was white hot. I tipped him backward to sit on the table. Instead of sitting on it, he laid down on his side and let the blood ooze from his mouth.

"What now? You guys got medicine?" I asked Shifty.

"No we don't got no damn medicine. Sneak him some hooch later."

"Soak his towel and pillowcase in cold water," I said.

"How about this, how about you soak them, fool," said Shifty. "Quitter."

"Hot Damn, soak his towel in cold water and bring it," I said.

Hot Damn did. A crowd formed around Mr. Clean on the table, like little people around Gulliver.

I walked gingerly to the portal bars. Two of the deputies remained watchful.

"He might need stitches to keep his eyebrows together," I said.

"Nurse comes back tomorrow morning," said one of the guys. I was swollen with adrenaline, and bleeding, and impervious to pain, and they saw me as Goliath. Or I hoped that's how they saw me. He said, "Why'd you quit?"

"I did what I needed to."

"What'd you need to do?" he said.

Deep breath.

Ow.

"I needed to earn it. You don't tell the sheriff, I won't either."

They both laughed, and told me I was a crazy son of a bitch, and one of them lost twenty bucks betting on Mr. Clean, and I went to run cold water over my knuckles.

22

Again I didn't sleep well. Every position hurt except laying on my back, and only serial killers did that. My hands throbbed too.

The next morning, Mr. Clean's breakfast was brought to him in his cell. He drank juice and sent the rest away. I drank coffee and juice, and ate the fruit.

The table of prisoners scrutinized everything I did. Not only had I beaten their king, I'd quit before claiming victory. I might be a crazy person. The best private cops don't accept the reward, I wanted to tell them.

Hot Damn didn't sit across from me. His position was unenviable. I'd saved his ass, and everyone knew it, and while they didn't resent him for it, he had to keep his distance from me or be seen as a bitch. Or something like that. Prison hierarchies were inscrutable.

The guy with the burgeoning afro had taken Hot Damn's seat.

"So you're like a cop," he said, like we hadn't been over this.

"For hire."

"But, man, you fight people."

"Only when..." Then again, I didn't know what the criteria was. And I was too tired to explain it. And my hands hurt. "If I have to."

"You had to fight Mr. Clean?"

"Maybe," I said.

"But most times, you help people."

"I try."

"I think I get it," he said.

I drank coffee.

He said, "You do stuff other people don't wanna? Right? And you said you told Big Willy to stop doing shit? And you fought Mr. Clean so Hot Damn didn't die. What it is is, you're like a guard."

"That's part of it."

"You're a wall that keeps bad stuff from nice people."

"Good observation," I said.

"Maybe I could do that. But..." He ate some eggs and screwed up one eye. "What's that go to do with bedtime? Why I gotta get up early?"

"That way, you'll be captive to nothing."

"Captive like in prison?" he said.

"No. Outside you need to fight against urges that will take you captive."

"Okay. Why?"

"To become the man you should be, you can't be addicted to booze or drugs or porn or laziness."

"Why not?" he said.

"Gotta be your own man, gotta be free. Go to bed early so you can get up early and do the work of being alive. And never let someone else wash your floors," I said.

He dropped his fork like he was angry. "Man, I don't get that shit. Go to bed and wash my floors? Why?"

"Life is chaos. Order it yourself."

"What?"

"If you don't, the prison has to," I said. "Do it yourself. Be a man, not a prisoner."

"Okay, yeah, but why?"

A banging at the portal bars.

"August! Let's go, you have a visitor." Deputy Cobb was shouting it.

"Thank God," I said.

Ronnie sat at a table in intake.

Her legs were crossed at the ankles under the table. Her skirt reached mid-calf, and she wore a matching blazer with notched collar and three-quarter sleeves. Small diamonds sparkled in her earlobes. Her hair was up in a braided bun. She wore no lipstick. She was making notes on a legal pad.

My breath was stolen. In only a few days, I'd forgotten how much Ronnie was.

She didn't look up.

"At the moment, Mackenzie, we are attorney and client. Do you understand?"

Her voice carried none of the warm jingle I knew.

I sat across from her and the table groaned.

The deputies watched us. No, they watched her.

"No promises, Ronnie."

"You're being interrogated by the detectives in a few minutes. I forced through a motion of discovery when the clerk's office opened so I could review the charges."

"Can you see the report on Maddie Owens?" I said.

"Yes. I have it."

"Tell me what you know."

She stopped making noses. She still wasn't looking at me.

"Maddie Owens shot herself in the head in the bedroom of her townhouse."

"How am I implicated?"

"Your..." She paused and tapped her pen three times on a blank spot of her legal pad. "Your DNA was found in her bed."

"My DNA?"

"The..." More tapping. "The kind of DNA found in bed after a sexual tryst."

"In Maddie's bed."

"Yes."

I felt like I'd been electrocuted.

"That's impossible," I said.

"There's more." With one hand, she slid a white paper loose, a photocopy of the report. They didn't let her bring her phone inside. "Before killing herself, Maddie recorded a short video on her phone. I haven't seen it yet, but here's the transcript. She was crying. She said she'd been having an affair with you, but that you grew jealous of her upcoming marriage and you threatened to expose the affair. That you confessed to her that you'd recently killed two men with a hammer, and that you would kill her too. Instead of facing the humiliation, she might kill herself. And if she did, she wanted the police to know why. She was found in her bed, gun in her hand. The gun is registered to you."

"My gun. In her hand."

"Yes."

"Jiminy Christmas."

Ronnie nodded.

I said, "My .38."

She consulted her paper.

"A Smith & Wesson .38 Special."

"How?" I closed my eyes to think. "*How?* That was in my glove compartment. Or my nightstand."

"Right now, that doesn't matter."

"My DNA could be located with an ultralight and transferred with a swab to Maddie's bed. Or hell, maybe simply she took our sheets."

"Mackenzie," she said.

"It's Helena. Our housekeeper had full access to our bedroom."

"*Mackenzie.*" Ronnie smacked her hand on the table. "This isn't the time. Helena didn't come along until the men were dead. No more fucking jokes."

"If you think I'd joke about having an affair, you've been doing a lot of not paying attention to me," I said.

"It *can't* be her."

"You're an attorney. You think in terms of black and white evidence, of what a jury would believe, of reasonable doubt. I'm an investigator. I know there's no such thing as coincidences. She's involved."

"At the moment, that's inconsequential. When speaking with the detectives, you say nothing. Your right to silence is invoked. As your—"

"You need to know," I said.

"I need to know what?"

"Ronnie. I didn't do this."

"I don't care if you're guilty or not. As your attorney, I'll never ask," she said.

"Ronnie. Ron."

She stared at her legal pad. Tap tap tap.

"I've never had an affair. And I never will," I said.

"That is not germane." The corners of her mouth threatened to turn down.

"I don't care about the rest of it. Any of it. Only us. You might have a fool for a client, but he's a fool in love with you. And he doesn't run around."

The tapping stopped.

She was crying.

I hated the idea of her agonizing all weekend about Maddie Owens, and then the trauma of seeing her worst-case-scenario this morning. My stomach churned with it.

I was going to break all of Green's teeth.

"I haven't seen Maddie in years."

She took a packet of tissues from her purse and pressed one to her eyes.

"We can't do this now," she said.

"I can't do anything else."

"Mackenzie." She spoke softly. "I decided over the weekend, if you and Maddie were involved sexually, I could forgive it. Probably. You've had to overlook a lot more."

I wanted to reply but couldn't.

"But..." She took the tissue away but kept her eyes closed. "If you had an affair, and you lie about it, and you go on making a fool out of me, that I won't be able to forgive."

"Ronnie."

"I can brave the embarrassment of the affair. I *think* I can. But I could not, and I will not, endure the pity that would come with further and unnecessary humiliation. I'm not a strong enough woman."

The intake room was stone silent. The television was muted. The deputies were eavesdropping, and so was the drunk in the corner. Ronnie was shatteringly beautiful when she cried.

"I don't lie to you," I said. "I don't ever."

She wasn't breathing.

I said, "It looks bad. I haven't seen the evidence but I believe you. I look guilty as hell. But I want you to put all the faith you possess in me."

A small nod. Or maybe it was my yearning for her to nod. I felt hot all over.

"I'm trying," she whispered. She was watching me now. Looking for signs. Looking for hope.

"I'll never cheat. Put your faith in me despite the evidence."

"I don't know how." She'd been keeping her hands away from me, but now she pressed them forward. I took them in mine. Hers perfect, mine the hands of a caveman.

"Trust my character. Remember that I've never lied to you. Or been cruel to you. Remember my promises."

"I do have faith in you, Mackenzie. I see that you're not lying. But..." She squeezed. "You were in her bed."

"Believe even when it doesn't make sense. Believe that the man I've been the past three years is the real man. Trust that my character is stronger than planted evidence."

She said, "Okay."

"Okay?"

"I'll try."

"That's what faith is. An act. A decision. A verb, like love."

"I want to," she said.

"Do it and we'll figure out the rest later."

She raised up, bolstered by an inner decision. "I'll jump. I'll believe you."

"I won't betray you."

"If you do... I think I'll be glad I made the leap anyway. I'll go down swinging."

"That's how I feel too. About us."

"I believe you." Another squeeze and she sniffed. "Saying it out loud helps. Mackenzie, your poor hands."

"Men are idiots, turns out."

"What happened?" she said.

"There was a big meanie."

"He attacked you?"

"He was gonna beat up another guy. I objected."

"Your fingers look awful. They're purple and cut open. Are they broken?" she said.

"My ribs are in bad shape, but otherwise I'm pristine. May I see the police reports?" I said.

She had all three—Jason Hicks, Donald Torres, and Maddie Owens. Without much time, I could only skim. Maddie Owens' body had been found a day before I was arrested, and she'd died a day before that, in the early afternoon, a Wednesday. While I'd been out researching the deaths of Jason and Donald.

Two items jumped out at me.

One, the hammer used to kill Hicks and Torres had been discovered inside Maddie's townhouse.

Absurd.

Two, a man's shirt had been discovered under Maddie's bed. The shirt was ripped, and it matched a torn patch of clothing found in Jason Hicks' bedroom, further linking the crime scenes.

Tooooooooo convenient.

"Does this not strike you as asinine? That I would leave all the evidence lying around?" I said. "It's absurd. I'm insulted."

"Green won't care. Nor will the Commonwealth's Attorney, nor a jury. They've got enough to put you away for life."

Yikes.

She said, "It's time. Green and Hart are interrogating you through a two-way mirror, on the first floor." She packed her pad and pen and tissues. "Also. Because it's me and because it's you, the Roanoke judges won't touch the case. They're recusing themselves. I scheduled a bond hearing with Judge Newman in Christiansburg for tomorrow morning, the earliest I could."

"I understand."

"Which means," she said, "at least one more night in jail."

"That's okay. Maybe we'll have squeeze dogs."

"Is that prison innuendo I shouldn't know about?"

"I wish." I indicated the photocopies of the crime scene reports. "Can I keep this?"

"I don't know that they'll let you."

I waved the papers at the deputy staring at Ronnie's ankles.

"I'm holding onto this. No staples, no paperclips."

The guy shrugged and said, "Whatever she says."

I folded the paper and shoved it into the pocket of my jumpsuit.

~

I sat on a stool. Green and Hart sat in chairs on the far side of the glass. Ronnie stood behind me.

Green asked questions for an hour. Archie Hart interjected softballs. They presented their evidence and conclusions and demanded explanations.

How long had you been dating Maddie Owens?

Where were you when she shot herself?

How'd she get your gun?

Why'd you leave your hammer there?

You know you're facing a life sentence?

You don't want to help us out?

Sentencing might go easier if you do.

Why Jason Hicks?

Were you two having a thing, like with Maddie?

Why Donald Torres?

Maybe you owed the Russians money?

How are Hicks and Torres related?

What should we tell their families?

Shouldn't Jason's parents have a reason? They lost their son, August.

We got you. You're toast. Red handed.

Did it have to do with your work?

Help us help you. Maybe your kid's in danger.

Is there anyone else?

Who else'd you kill, August? Better you tell us now.

Who else?

They got nowhere.

In the glass I could see the ghost of Ronnie's reflection behind me. Her arms were crossed and she glared through me. A wife and an attorney, praying her career and her marriage weren't both going up in flames.

My client has no comment.

No comment.

My client invokes his Fifth Amendment right.

My client won't answer that.

My client maintains his innocence.

My client maintains his innocence.

My client...

My client.
My husband.
My husband wouldn't do that.
My husband wouldn't make a fool out of me.
He wouldn't embarrass me.
He claims he's innocent.
His DNA was in her bed...
But my husband says he's innocent.
Despite all appearances.
My husband maintains his innocence.

~

MUCH WAS SAID that wasn't said.

The questions insulted me and implied she was too stupid to know the truth. It wasn't just me being interrogated.

When the detectives finished, my deputy returned to walk me upstairs. Ronnie squeezed my arm and she left at a businesswoman's clip.

23

The next morning.

I arrived at the garage at seven, handcuffed and escorted by two yawning deputies, and Manny was waiting. Marshals transport prisoners. Our friendship constituted an enormous conflict of interest, but Marshal Warren wouldn't push Deputy Martinez on it. He took possession, unlocked the cuffs and let them drop to the garage floor, and put me in the back of my own Honda Accord. Sheriff Stackhouse arrived from her office and ducked into the front passenger seat, and Manny reversed from the prison and into the wild world.

A gusty Tuesday morning. The first time I'd seen the sky since Friday. It was much as I remembered.

"You took terrible in orange." Manny was looking at me in the rearview.

"It's off the rack, too. Humiliating."

"You got a boyfriend now?" he said.

"No. But the line is long and eager."

Stackhouse twisted enough to set a hand on my knee. "You look too big back there. Did you sleep?"

"Some," I said.

"What do you think of my prison?"

"Your cooks should be transferred to death row."

Manny detoured through a Dunkin' Donuts and ordered me a bacon and egg sandwich, two donuts, and coffee with cream.

I could not love Manny so much
Loved I not honor more.

"Veronica's already there," said Stackhouse.

In response, I ate the Bismark in one bite.

"Are they still making prison hooch?" she said.

"You think I'm a snitch."

"Someone did—I heard you beat the hell out of Mr. Clean, and everyone got drunk."

"I cannot confirm that."

"Babe. Don't talk with your mouth full."

Manny said, "Ay, Mr. Clean? I put him in there. *Gran tonto*. He was an enforcer for a bike gang in North Carolina. Before he met me."

"I think he broke my ribs."

"And your hands?" said Stackhouse.

"I broke them. Against his *tonto* face."

"I lost a hundred dollars betting against Mr. Clean last month," she said. "He's a monster."

"He's a kitten now."

She smiled and turned around. "I may have to move you to higher security, on the fourth floor. For the safety of my other inmates."

~

THE MONTGOMERY COUNTY COURTHOUSE had been redesigned in the past decade. Now the building looked like an upscale movie theater with towering windows. Lacking the austerity and gravitas of a classic courthouse, the place looked cheap, like it was trying too hard.

Stackhouse and Manny were much caressed and fawned over by the security guards and the courthouse staff. Ronnie joined us in the waiting room. She said good morning and sat in the chair opposite me and crossed her legs and flipped through pages of the Virginia Code.

We waited alone, the four of us, and I was struck by the solemnity of my escorts. Ronnie, Manny, and Stackhouse were prone to be jocose and flippant, no matter the situation. Not today. They sat quietly, eyes on the courtroom door.

A circuit judge was not to be taken lightly.

A bailiff knocked on the doorframe and led us into the courtroom. The judge was a woman who looked like the aunt you didn't like, with something close to a perm, and she watched us over her bifocals. The Montgomery County commonwealth's attorney was an unfamiliar man dressed in a dark blue suit one size too small, and a hundred dollars too cheap, and he was mostly bald and he was sweating.

"Good morning, counselors," said Judge Newman.

She didn't sound like it was a good morning.

"Good morning, Your Honor," said Veronica Summers.

I remained standing and essaying innocence.

"Sheriff," said the judge. "Nice to see you."

"You too, sweetie." Stackhouse smiled. "I mean, Judge Newman."

Without moving much, Newman indicated me with her pen. "This is the gentleman causing all the trouble."

"Alleged gentleman, Your Honor," said Ronnie, and

everyone chuckled. Jokes were risky, because if they didn't land then you were already behind. Hers had landed.

"Well. Let's begin. I have a motion from Ms. Summers asking for bond," said the judge. Her voice was a trumpet without effort. A trumpet tuned finely to drown out other noises. She was a largish woman and filled the bench well.

"Yes, Your Honor."

"Mr. Burton, are you prepared to move forward?"

The bald man nodded. "I am."

"Ms. Summers, call your first witness or proceed by proffer."

A motion asking for bond was essentially a minor trial, with a verdict reached immediately. The crime wasn't on trial—my character was. My freedom would be the verdict. Should I be released unto the wide Earth until my criminal trial, or should I be sent back to my cell to wait for months?

Ronnie called Stackhouse to the stand, and then Manny, both esteemed members within law enforcement circles. From them she secured testimony that I wasn't a flight risk, I presented no danger to myself or my family, I was an upstanding member of my community, and I had no criminal history.

Mr. Burton cross-examined, but only to establish their close relationship—even cohabitation—with me. The implication was, their testimony was biased.

After twenty minutes of stating the obvious, that I was second only to Abraham Lincoln himself, Ronnie said, "No further evidence, Your Honor. We ask for bond."

"Very well, Ms. Summer. Does the Commonwealth wish to present evidence?" said the judge.

Prosecutor Burton stood.

"The Commonwealth only presents the crime scene

report from the home of Maddie Owens, Your Honor. Roanoke City Police reports that Maddie died from a gunshot wound to the head, and that it was Mr. August's gun."

Ronnie stood too.

"Objection, Your Honor. It was *allegedly* Mr. August's gun. And that's irrelevant, because Roanoke City Police did not charge my client with using a firearm," she said.

Burton drummed his fingers on his desk and rejoined, "In considering bond, the judicial officer shall consider whether a firearm was allegedly used in the commission of the offense. A firearm *was* allegedly used in the commission. Taking Maddie Owens' death in connection with the other two homicides—"

"*Objection*, Your Honor. Mr. Burton is referencing facts of the case beyond the scope of bail. We are *not* here to discuss facts of the case, and the prosecution should remember that," said Ronnie.

Burton's face pinked.

Judge Newman's eyes flicked between them. "Mr. Burton, the court notes that Maddie Owens allegedly killed herself with a firearm, but it holds no bearing at the bond trial for Mr. August."

"Yes, Your Honor."

Newman turned her cold, pale, reptilian gaze on me, over the cut of her bifocals.

"Mr. August."

I stood.

"Your Honor."

"Do you maintain your innocence?" she said.

"I do."

"Why do you need to be out on bond?"

"To catch the person who killed Jason Hicks and Donald Torres," I said.

The gallery behind us rumbled with amusement. We'd drawn a crowd far larger than most motions.

Judge Newman didn't want to smile but she did.

"You intend to catch the killer of Jason Hicks and Donald Torres, Mr. August," she said.

"I will."

"Two men you are accused of killing," she said.

"That lends urgency to my efforts."

"I imagine it does. How do you intend to do that?"

"It's what I do for a living. I investigate," I said.

"What will you investigate?"

"The evidence. Much of it is being ignored. Your Honor."

"Ignored?"

"Yes ma'am," I said.

"In my experience I haven't found that detectives ignore evidence. In my experience, experts can be trusted."

"I don't necessarily trust experts. I trust good people," I said.

"Are..." She paused to look at her notes. "Are Detectives Green and Hart not good people?"

"They got this one way wrong. Your honor."

"Way wrong."

I nodded.

Beside me, Ronnie was so tight I could hear her muscles squeaking.

Judge Newman smiled to herself again. "Way wrong."

"Yes ma'am."

"To investigate, you'll be driving all over kingdom come?"

"Possibly," I said. "I work hard."

"Are you willing to subject yourselves to pretrial services?"

"I am, though I need to leave the state."

Ronnie made a small groan.

"Leave the state?" Judge Newman looked deeply displeased. "Why?"

"Some of the evidence that the detectives refuse to investigate leads there."

"Where?"

"New York and New Jersey," I said.

"What evidence leads there?"

"Donald Torres is not his real name. His real name was Danil Turgenev. There's strong evidence to suggest he's former Russian Mafia. I found phone numbers and addresses from his old life, and I intended to pursue them before Detective Green arrested me."

The judge was silent a long time. I counted to twenty in my head.

"Not his real name."

"No ma'am," I said.

"Can you prove that?"

"Easily."

"Did you say the Russian Mafia?"

"I did."

"Sounds like a spy novel."

"Doesn't it."

"Does Roanoke City have this evidence?"

"They should, but thus far I haven't been impressed. I found the evidence and handed it to them," I said.

"How'd you do that?"

"I'm good at my job. Your Honor."

"Be specific."

"Detectives Green and Hart couldn't find Donald Torres' office. I did. The evidence of his former life was on the computer. I found the evidence, including his passport."

"You said you turned the evidence over," she said.

"Yes. To Detective Green."

"And?"

"He was confounded."

"Confounded," she said.

"Yes ma'am."

"And now you want to investigate your discoveries," she said.

"Yes ma'am."

"Out of the state. In New York."

"Yes ma'am," I said.

"If I grant bond, you'd need to wear an ankle monitor, to track your whereabouts. Would you be willing?"

"Certainly. I'll even take you with me, if you like."

More amusement from the gallery.

Ronnie was going to hit me soon.

Judge Newman leaned back in her chair, the first time she'd done that, and she laughed.

"That won't be necessary, Mr. August, but I appreciate your willingness."

"Yes ma'am."

"Ms. Summers," she said. "Mr. August is your husband."

"Yes, Your Honor."

"He seems a handful."

"And he's innocent," said Ronnie.

"I'm not sure it's wise to represent your spouse, Counselor."

"She who represents herself has a fool for a client,

your honor. But she who represents her husband would be a fool to do otherwise. No one cares about this case more than me," said Ronnie.

"You agree to these pretrial services? The ankle monitor?" said the judge.

"Yes, Your Honor, we do."

"Very well. Bond is granted, for one-hundred-thousand dollars. Mr. August, don't make me regret this decision," said Judge Newman.

With the light hammering of her gavel, my freedom was restored.

24

For the sake of appearances, I let Manny drive my Honda on the return trip. That, and he wouldn't give me the keys.

Back in Roanoke, at the jail, I changed into my personal clothes and Deputy Cobb affixed a thick black band to my ankle. The monitor would track me through a GPS service and check my sweat once an hour. I was processed out of prison and I left through the front doors, a man who could eat where he pleased and walk where he willed.

We lunched at Billy's and I drank the best lager of my life. Ronnie sat beside me and I sensed her hesitancy. She trusted me, but it was the same trust one placed in a rickety wooden bridge. Yes, it would probably hold, but one must proceed with caution and a racing pulse...

Faith didn't mean unconditional marital bliss. If the situation was reversed, I'd be uncertain too.

After lunch, my coterie left for their jobs and I picked my son up early from school. The front receptionist had clearly heard of my incarceration, because her face tightened until I thought it might tear, and she excused herself to make a phone call—probably Ronnie—and when she brought Kix she did so as though she'd never see him again, tears in her eyes.

Kix, though, had no uncertainty. He was with his father.

Dad, he said in the car. Giant blue eyes, fat cheeks in the mirror. *Dad Dad Dad Dad.*

"Yes?" I said. "Yes yes yes?"

I'm relieved you returned. My grandfather tried to read me a book but he fell asleep. Can you believe that? An ADULT. He may stay up late as he wants, but he fell to snoring in the rocking chair! What an abuse of privilege. When I am an adult, I will probably never sleep. Manny has been a chore since you've been gone, like his dog died, believe me. Momma's been squeezing me too tight. Did you hear me? Daddy. She's been hugging me like I'm a stuffed bear, and kissing me and crying, and, frankly, I'm tired of supporting the entire family. Oh! And get THIS! Charlotte tried to kiss me today! KISS me? Dad? Dad Dad Dad! Did you hear? Her MOUTH, on my FACE. Did I give consent? No I did not. No means no, but then she started crying, and I had to tattle on her. I didn't want to, but right is right and wrong is wrong. Also my snacks have been abysmal. Let's work on this as a family.

We drove to the Wasena Park and Kix talked the whole time about anything and everything, bringing up sex more than once, and I pushed him on the swing until he tired and threatened to nod off, so we motored home and took a nap together in my bed, my enormous soft bed, my mattress more than a cot, and the guy next door wasn't crying, and I was happy.

"THE CRIMINAL CHARGES MATTER," I declared that night after dinner. I'd cooked flounder, mussels, and shrimp in a white wine and butter sauce, with angel hair pasta. The customary gathered host, pliant now sated, listened intensely. "But so do the civil implications. I did not kill those men, and I did not have an affair with Maddie Owens. You haven't asked, but I'm informing you anyway. I'm a one-woman guy. I found mine, and she's it. For life. My DNA didn't get to any of those crime scenes organically. It was planted. I'll figure out how soon. The police detectives might tittup through the evidence, but I won't. That is all."

Stackhouse, sitting at the opposite end of the table, raised her glass of red.

"We never doubted you, babe."

"And if you did kill them," said Manny, "so what. You earned a few, way I see it."

"Not the way Judge Newman would, though."

"Will no one ask what tittup means?" said Timothy.

Manny shook his head. "No. That's what he wants."

I ran my finger on the table.

"No streaks," I said.

"Olga comes tomorrow to butcher the place and ruin our happiness, *aya yay*."

"Helena," said Ronnie.

Manny cracked a second can of Dogfish Head Slightly Mighty IPA—low carb, like a sissy—and poured it into a glass.

"Why do you protect her so much, *señorita*?"

"I'm not sure." Ronnie's voice still carried no lilt. Ronnie herself hadn't eaten with us, not really; she'd sent her exhausted representative instead, less likely to be humiliated and hurt.

"Because she's a cute blonde, like you?" said Manny.

"Maybe."

"I thought she lost her hair due to cancer and radiation?" I said.

"It's growing back. And her eyebrows aren't dark," said Manny.

"I think it's because," said Ronnie and she took the napkin from her lap to wipe her mouth, though it wasn't necessary. She folded the blue cloth and set it down again. "In part, I see myself in Helena. She's a small woman, alone in the world, doing her best. She has cancer but no one to care for her. If I had cancer a few years ago, my situation would've been similar. Alone and sick and sad."

A sobering thought, and none of us replied.

GPA sat next to her, expressing sororal concern.

She said, "I cannot muster up any suspicion of Helena."

"But, son, you still believe she's involved?" said Timothy.

"Yes, though now I feel bad about it."

Timothy stood and picked up his plate and the plate of his paramour. "Well, she comes tomorrow. Helena does. Nine in the morning. If possible, please interrogate her without running her off. I'm enjoying our clean bathroom."

"You know." Stackhouse tilted her head upward to gaze into the ceiling, at the unseen master bath. "Now that Mackenzie mentioned it, I've paid attention. The girl doesn't do as good a job as I thought."

"Can you blame her? She's dying. Or she came close to it," said Timothy.

"Exactly," Ronnie said.

"What if," said Manny, "I give her a hundred dollars a week to not clean our house?"

"I'll match it," I said.

Ronnie stood. Her blue napkin fell to the floor. She took Kix under his arms and hoisted him from his high chair.

"Kix needs a bath," she said, and she took him up, soft footfalls on the steps.

GPA whined at me.

"I know," I said. My heart hurt and I rubbed her between the ears. "I'm working on it."

I FINISHED BRUSHING MY TEETH.

Ronnie was reading in bed, a Boo Walker novel. Her back was propped against the wooden headboard and she was very slightly squinting at the pages. I bet she'd need reading glasses within the year.

"Today was hard," I said.

She closed the book.

"For you. Not for me," I said. "It was good for me."

"It was a mixture of both. I'm glad you're out of prison."

"People are treating you with kid gloves?" I said.

"They won't look at me. It's maddening. And humiliating. But it's understandable. I wouldn't know how to treat my paralegal if she was sleeping with an alleged murderer."

"Everyone knows?"

"It's all anyone talks about," she said.

"I'm sorry."

"It's not your fault."

"That doesn't mean I don't hate it for you," I said.

"Thank you."

I wore pajama pants and a white T-shirt.

"I know that people aren't just one thing. That it's possible to trust me, and to also not trust me at the same time. To know I'm innocent, but to feel like I'm a stranger," I said.

"It's more like..." She swallowed. "I don't know either of us."

"A lonely hollow feeling."

"I trust you, Mackenzie. And I'll love you always."

"But there's still a chance I'm dissembling. And that small drop of uncertainty can spoil the rest," I said.

She looked at her knees.

I took my pillow off the bed. "I'm sleeping on the floor."

"I'm not asking you to do that. This is our bed."

"I know. I don't want you to be alone, but I don't want to pressure you. The floor is fine."

"Ay, it's better than fine," said Manny. He lay on his air mattress at my feet, a novel flat on his chest. "Get down here, *hombre*."

Ronnie grinned. She had relaxed, knowing I wouldn't force intimacy.

"Did you sleep here every night?" I said.

"*Por supuesto*. I didn't want her to be alone either."

"Helps that she's a hot blonde," I said.

"Helps me every day. Also her snoring puts me to sleep."

"I do not snore," said Ronnie.

"Her cute normal breathing puts me to sleep."

I selected three blankets from our hall closet and lay

one of them down as padding beside Manny. I lowered with a grunt.

"It's way down here."

"*Bienvenidos*," said Manny.

"Are people treating you differently?" I said.

"I don't care about people. Also. You can sleep with me but you can't talk, *bien*?"

"*No hay pedo*."

Manny prayed. "*Padre celestial, gracias por Mack. Ayúdalo mañana a atrapar a un asesino. Ayuda a la bella Ronnie a dormir bien. En tu nombre de Jesucristo, amén*."

"Amen."

Ronnie turned out the light and the three of us lay in the warm dark and the ambient sounds.

Manny was asleep within sixty seconds.

In Kix's room, GPA repositioned herself on the dog bed and sighed. Through the slats in our window, the dappled moon passed beyond the leaves of the maple tree in our front yard. The refrigerator cycled on in the kitchen as I watched the window, and when I breathed deeply I inhaled the flavors of Manny—Argan oil, luxury night cream for his face, and minty toothpaste.

Ronnie and I were both awake an hour later, not speaking. I listened to the sounds of her eyelids opening and closing, and finally her cute normal breathing, and it was the best I could do.

25

I drove Kix to school, and the front receptionist released a breath she'd been holding all night. I hadn't eaten my son.

I returned home and poured another cup of coffee and reclined in the leather reading chair by the front door. Just me and GPA, waiting.

To catch a housekeeper. Chris Hansen would be proud. Helena would walk in and I'd spring my trap—ah *hah*, show me the adulterant you use on my floors, and the ultraviolet light you use to scan my bed.

Nine came and went.

Still we waited. I played Wordle on my phone, and found a repository of older Wordles and beat those too.

Nine-thirty.

I thought about the Masters, which had been played two weekends ago, and debated whether I still had time to become a professional golfer. I was a big guy, better built for hitting running backs foolish enough to come through the A gap. But Bryson DeChambeau was biggish, and he could hit a golf ball. I hadn't played in a year, but probably if I applied myself real hard...

At ten o'clock, I called my father.

"She's not here. You're sure this was the day?"

"It should be. This was the day we agreed on," he said.

"Send me her phone number."

"I don't have it. We worked out the arrangement in person," he said.

"What's the arrangement?"

"She comes in the morning, after I'm gone for work. I leave cash. When she's done, she writes a note saying she'll be back next week, Wednesday usually."

Wednesday. Maddie Owens was killed Wednesday afternoon, DNA planted in her bed. Freshly swabbed from mine?

"You have no way to contact her," I said.

"I don't. It seems a little silly, now."

"In fact," I said, "it does."

I hung up and waited another hour.

No Helena the housekeeper.

~

Two of the addresses I found on Donald Torres' computer were in Brighton Beach and a third in Coney Island—all three located on the coast of Brooklyn, only a few miles apart.

Manny drove in his black supercharged Camaro. Seated in the passenger seat, I pretended I wasn't saying the Lord's Prayer over and over and contemplating mortality. The seven-hour drive took four and a half, and we arrived before dinner.

The neighborhoods were a mixture of cheap beach tourism and Russian milieu, active and loud. The addresses in Brighton Beach each led us to an auto repair shop, one mile apart. We glared at them and willed them to give up their secrets, but the mechanics kept being mechanics. The Coney Island address was a high-rise apartment building. I took photos of everything, as per my defense attorney's instructions.

The New York air coming off the Lower Bay was cold and damp, and I shivered in the shadows of the Coney Island tower and read the names on the call box and saw no Torres or Turgenev. I pushed a handful of buttons and asked for Donald Torres or Danil Turgenev and was told over and over that I had the wrong unit. The superintendent told me to stop being an ass and I flashed my badge but he said he'd never heard of a Danil Turgenev.

We drove back to Brighton Beach and ordered lamb kebabs from the Kashkar Cafe and ate them while watching an auto shop close down. I wondered if somewhere a correctional officer was staring at my location on a digital map, worried silly about the ankle monitor.

Manny phoned his office, but they'd left for the day. He called Beck's cell, who called someone else, and she got the personal number of a deputy marshal in Brooklyn, who put Manny in touch with an organized crime police unit. We spoke to Sergeant Popov on speaker.

"We need information about an auto shop," I said, and I read him the address.

"Yah I know the shop," said Popov. He had an accent like a Russian raised at Yankee games. "That's Nikitin's shop. At night you run down the oil steps and play the high-stakes poker, you want."

"In the oil well of a mechanic?"

"It's nice. The guy, he runs a good game," said Popov.

"Is Nikitin Russian Mafia?"

"Nikitin's a Brigadier, or *Avtoritet*, in a family

connected to the Bratva. He runs the poker in Brighton. This guy, he's on your shit list?"

"Not him," I said. "We're looking for information on Danil Turgenev. Some evidence leads to this shop."

"Turgenev. Turgenev. Never heard of this guy," said Popov. "Danil Turgenev."

"Turgenev was a largely unknown entity, and he's dead now, found in Virginia. Here's my theory—Turgenev pissed off the Russians. Most likely the mafia, especially with my address leading to an underground casino. Maybe it was money, maybe it's something else. Whatever it was, he had to be gone in a hurry but he didn't run far enough."

"This happens a lot. Cross the wrong gopnik or the boss, you're a dead man. Russian on Russian violence is out of control. Bratok's are thick on the pavement, ready for hire," said our phone.

"Is Nikitin a powerful enough guy to scare Turgenev away?" I said.

"He's a powerful guy, yah, but... Nikitin, he's one guy out of a lot of guys. You understand? The group, they call themselves Thieves-in-Law. Could be Nikitin, could be another guy like him. Nikitin works for... No, how do I say it. He works *under* Obshchak. A group of Russian overseers."

"I want to know who killed Turgenev. And who ordered it."

Popov laughed and it was at my expense.

"I don't know we have informants that deep, comrade. And please listen to me. You go into a place like Nikitin's casino and ask, you do not come out. The Russian, they are not good people."

"Aren't you Russian?" I said.

"That is how I know. I am not good people either."

I read him the address of the residential high-rise, and he said a thousand Russians lived there, probably some in the mafia, but nobody of consequence.

I said I might call him back and we hung up.

"Organized crime guy never heard of your boy, Daniel Turgy-whatever," said Manny.

"Means Donald wasn't a big player. He might be a normal guy who ran up a big tab at the casino."

"Then why'd you kill him?"

"Great question," I said.

~

WE DROVE to Newark with one hour of daylight left.

The first addresses took us to a mud pit, out of which new steel construction rose. The mud pit was surrounded by small houses, and the safe bet was, Donald's address was a house that no longer existed. It'd been bulldozed within the past six months.

The second address was an accounting firm inside a strip mall, sandwiched between a Buffalo Wild Wings and sushi joint. Glass front, shingled roof, not enough parking. Lights were on inside.

I knocked on the glass door of the accounting firm and I stepped inside.

No one shot me.

I stood listening near the reception desk in a waiting area with two chairs and nothing to read. No one appeared, so I wandered to the hallway beyond. A woman worked at a desk in the second office. She was smallish, Black, with tight cornrows and she wore a pink button-down shirt with high collar. Her nails matched the pink shirt. When she saw me, she jumped and said, “Oh shit.”

I waved like I was friendly, not a mafia hitman.

“Sorry. I knocked but…”

“We closed,” she said.

“You’re working late.”

“Tax season.” She made an apologetic smile. “I should have locked the front door. Please come back tomorrow.”

I fished out my wallet, and her eyes rounded and she watched, assuming my wallet would be a gun, but it wasn’t. I flashed the badge and the license, and she didn’t seem mollified.

“I’m looking for Daniel Turgenev.”

“Mr. Turgenev? Why you looking for him?” she said.

“I have reasons. Important reasons. The best reasons.”

“Well, he’s gone. Matter fact, this used to be his office. I took it.”

“Where’d he go?”

“Shit, I don’t know. Nobody does. Probably he’s dead and he’ll float up in a year,” she said.

“Float up.”

“That’s what I said.”

“Means you think he’s dead. And it wasn’t an accident.”

“Listen, I don’t think you’re a cop. I think you’re lying, and I want you the hell out,” she said. “You see my finger?”

I did.

“It’s a great one,” I said. Her hand was resting on her office phone.

“You think I’m playing?”

“I do not.”

“That’s right. And my finger’s on the speed dial button. I push it and it calls 911. You don’t leave right this damn second, I'm pushing it. Because nobody who worked with Mr. Turgenev was any good, and we're glad his ass is gone, so don't you come around here pretending to be a cop."

"I am a cop. A private one. But I'll leave right this damn second." I slid one of my cards out of the wallet and let it drop to the floor. "You're right, Danil Turgenev is dead. In Virginia. And I want to know who did it. If you think of anything, call that number."

"I'm not going to."

I stepped backward out of her office, into the hallway. "I believe you. He was a tax accountant?"

"Shady as all get-out, too," she said. "No surprise to anyone he's dead."

"Who were his clients?"

"Up yours."

"This is helpful."

She faked a smile.

I saluted her.

"Good luck with tax season."

"*Good bye,*" she said.

Ah, northern manners, a cool breath of fresh air.

26

"Danil Turgenev was a shady accountant in a world of shady Russians, and he frequented shady places like underground poker rooms, and it's no surprise to the people who knew Danil that he's dead," I said.

Breakfast in the August household was not a leisurely, sit-down affair. It was a pour yourself a coffee and sprint affair. Because even when we got up early, and we usually did, we visited the gym or went jogging, or did something that put us behind the eight-ball.

I had Ronnie and Stackhouse and Timothy in the kitchen for only a hot minute, and I was talking fast.

"He was cooking books for the Russian mob?" said Stackhouse.

"Or stealing from them, or going into debt, or something else ill-advised. A cop up there said if I went asking questions about it, I'd be dead too."

"After your hearing yesterday, Judge Newman called the police chief," said Stackhouse. "She wanted to know why Donald Torres' fake identity hadn't been investigated, and the chief was humiliated. Detectives Green and Hart are catching hell, I hear, being accused of promotion-hunting for busting the famous private detective."

"I hope they're transferred to Siberia." Timothy was listening while he packed teacher evaluations into a leather briefcase. "Putting my only begotten son into prison."

"About Helena. She didn't show up yesterday."

"Do you still believe she's involved?" he said. "With organized crime from New York? She's been cleaning the neighbors for years."

"How do you know?" I said.

"She provided a list of references. The neighbors themselves."

"Did you call?"

"I did." Timothy smiled, pleased to have done something right. "The Burns family and Ms. Ortega. I called them both. They gave glowing recommendations."

"Do you still have the numbers?"

"I threw them away. But the Burns live around the corner, and Ms. Ortega is across the street from them, I think," he said.

"Georgina Princess and I will wait for Helena again. Maybe she got her days confused."

"I have to run." Ronnie was looking at her watch.

"Me too," said Stackhouse.

Ronnie kissed me on the cheek and said, "Keep me updated. Stay away from any Russians."

And then, as though taken by a tornado, they were gone, off to jobs where they weren't accused of murder and malfeasance.

Must be nice.

AT TEN, I deduced Helena wasn't coming. Again.

AWOL two days in a row?

If I was wrong and she wasn't a villainous housekeeper, then she could be a victim. She might be dead, somehow involved with the mob.

I pulled on my black North Face windbreaker and entered the neighborhood. The cherry trees had shed their bridal pink, and oak trees were budding green. My yard needed to be mowed before next week, and Wendell Berry would be pleased to learn I'd do it myself, rather than hire a specialist.

Me and Johnny Appleseed, two peas in an American pod. Except as I walked my left ankle clunked with a GPS monitor.

On Maiden Lane, I knocked on the Burns' door and Mrs. Burns answered, bright as the sun and beaming, clearly ignorant of my charges, else she might've shot me. She was dressed in athletic gear, like she could burst into a 5K any second, her hair up, and I knew Ronnie would be comparing Mrs. Burns' leg muscles to her own.

"Hiya, Mackenzie!" She was married to a gynecologist and she had no children of her own, providing wide margin for neighborliness.

"Mrs. Burns, good—"

"I *told* you, call me Peachy."

"I will not," I said.

"Everyone does!"

"Peachy Burns? I can't."

"Pooh on you, Mackenzie," she said. "Did I tell you I read your story in the newspaper?"

"Be serious, no one reads the newspaper. Mrs. Burns, I'm worried about Helena."

"Helena?" If Peachy hadn't injected her face with Botox every three months, she'd look confused.

"We share a housekeeper, I was told. Helena."

"Oh *her*! Is something wrong?" said Peachy.

"She didn't show up, two days in a row. I'm dismayed. You know, with the cancer..." I spread my hands, like *—maybe the worst has happened? Should we check on her?*

"Oh dear. Oh wow."

"Do you have her number?" I said.

"I didn't know she had *cancer*."

"Did—"

"And wait, Helena's not her name. It's María."

"María."

Peachy nodded, thrilled.

"Shame on you, Mackenzie, forgetting the help's name."

"Pooh on me."

"That's *right*," she said. "I didn't know she cleaned for you!"

"My father Timothy said he called for a reference. That's why our housekeeper was hired, on the strength of your referral."

"Maybe he spoke to my husband?"

"Have you seen María recently?"

"Sure! Two days ago."

"How'd her hair look?" I said.

"*Gorgeous*. I've told her she could sell it for a *fortune*." She pivoted and indicated the inside of her house. "Come in, Mackenzie."

"Mrs. Burns—"

"Peachy!"

"Mrs. Burns, is María Latina?" I said.

"Of course, silly."

"Have you ever employed a Caucasian housekeeper?"

"No I don't think they do that, do they?" she said. "Please come in, Mackenzie, and I'll pour mimosas. Confession, it'll be my third! Is Veronica around? I *adore* her, you know."

Before Ronnie, Peachy Burns would've knocked my hat off. I would've taken as much of her as I could get. Now though...

"I need to find my housekeeper. You're on your own, with the mimosas."

"If you *insist,* Mackenzie. But come back and tell me about the cancer girl soon."

"You bet."

I jogged across the street and knocked on Ms. Ortega's door. Mr. Bradley answered and explained I'd woken him from his morning nap, and Ms. Ortega lived one house *over*. I did my best to look sheepish and I knocked on the real Ms. Ortega's door.

"Ms. Ortega, do you have a housekeeper?" I said.

Ms. Ortega liked to walk the neighborhood dressed too warm, sometimes carrying weights. Now, standing in her doorway, she looked older. "No and I'm not in the market for one, and you're too big to do the job well anyway."

"When did you last have a housekeeper?"

"I never did and I never will. Do you think my arms are broken?" she said.

I grinned.

"Atta girl. Wash your own floors."

"Don't atta girl me."

"Has my father ever called you?" I said.

"Who is your father?"

"Timothy August, one street over. Looks like a weatherman."

"I know him by sight. He has never called me and he's too young for me anyway."

"Do you know anyone named Helena?" I said.

"My sister."

"Is she much...ah... How old is she?"

"She's eighty-eight come July," said Ms. Ortega.

"I'm sorry to bother you, ma'am," I said and she shut the door. Across the street, Peachy was sitting on her front steps, her legs crossed and kicking and she waved at me.

"Any luck?" she called.

"None."

"Oh pooh. Can I tempt you with the mimosa now?"

"Almost," I said. "But I adore Veronica even more than you do, and I need to call her."

"What a darling husband you are. So well trained!"

The next time I walked GPA, I might let her pooh in the Burns' yard.

~

I DID BETTER than call Ronnie. I drove to her office.

Her law firm kept the top floor in a renovated brick building off Salem Avenue. I pushed open the heavy wooden door, and her receptionist/paralegal made a little gasp behind her broad desk. Katie Drake taught elementary for three years before burning out, the poor thing, and she returned to college to earn a paralegal certificate.

She looked like Maggie Gyllenhaal if Maggie didn't have a team of beauticians.

"Good morning, Katie."

"Good morning, Mr. August." She said it without moving her lips. Frozen.

"I'm here to kill you."

Her skin was splotching. "That's *not* funny."

"You're right," I said. "Consider it retracted. Is her highness in?"

In the inner office, Ronnie sat at her big L-shaped desk, bent over spreadsheet printouts. I knocked on her door. She looked up and took off her reading glasses.

"I didn't know you wore reading glasses," I said. "Or if I did, I thought they were decoration, though I recently wondered if you needed them."

"They became a necessity. I didn't want to tell you."

"Why not?"

"For fear you might trade me in for a newer model," she said.

"I would marry you if you were ninety-five."

"What if I was ninety-six?"

"Ew, gross," I said.

Ronnie smiled.

"Helena doesn't exist," I said.

"I beg your pardon?"

"Our housekeeper. She's not real."

"I've met her. Twice," said Ronnie.

"The list of references she provided? Bogus. I walked to our neighbors' houses and inquired, and they've never heard of a Helena. When my father called the fake references, he spoke to actors who gave him a glowing report. That's why she's awful at cleaning—she's not a cleaner."

Ronnie stood as though levitating.

"Then... Who is she?"

"My guess, a professional killer for the Russian mafia.

We have no way to reach her. And I suspect she's long gone," I said.

"The cancer?"

"A deception, probably, to pull at Timothy's heartstrings."

"Why would... Why would someone...?"

"She worked hard to get into our house. Cleaning was a trojan horse, to get my gun or my DNA. Or something worse. We were sabotaged from within," I said.

"Oh Mackenzie." Ronnie came around the desk, barefoot. She put her around me and squeezed, her face against my chest. "Oh Mackenzie, I'm so sorry."

"The fault is not yours."

"But I didn't believe you. I defended her, instead of... She's an *imposter*. I'm embarrassed, Mackenzie."

"Defending the weak is not a bad character trait," I said.

She released me and stepped back. She was seeing the whole thing anew, from a different angle. Her eyes, a shade bluer than hazel depending on the light, were full of motions and evidence.

"Mackenzie. You were framed."

"I was. You knew this," I said.

"I know, but... You *really* were. This is wild. Someone who wanted to hurt you was in our bedroom."

"She swabbed the sheets. That's where she got DNA to plant at Maddie Owens' place," I said.

Ronnie took my face in her hands. Went up on her tiptoes and kissed me on the mouth. She was reborn with confirmation of my innocence.

"Mackenzie."

"Yes Ronnie."

"I knew you didn't kill those men. And I knew you

didn't cheat on me. But seeing it now as fact set in stone, it's..."

I picked her up and we kissed a long moment. We'd never broken but we'd bent, only for a few days, and we held together. Perhaps stronger for it.

"I'm beyond relieved." She wasn't crying. But she wasn't not crying either. "I feel like I was lost but now I'm not."

"Welcome back."

"I'm shaking, Mackenzie. I didn't realize how scared I was until now. The release of tension."

"Is your paralegal prudish?"

"She is. Nearly puritanical."

"Then I won't lay you on the couch and consummate the release of tension. I'll be respectful and wait," I said.

She wiggled her hips against mine.

"Can you wait?"

"Not if you keep doing that," I said.

"I'm not sure I could anyway. I feel weak." She held up her hand, which trembled. "With desire, of course."

"Obviously."

She kissed me once more and stepped away, returning to her profession. She wiped her eyes and took a deep breath and walked to her window and back.

"There are enough oddities to this case that I could convince a jury there's reasonable doubt. I'd bet my career you'd be found not guilty. But I don't want to win a trial. I want these counterfeit charges dropped."

"We need to find Helena, then," I said.

"Unless she's a fool, she fled Roanoke."

"And she's not one."

"The question remains, how was your DNA planted at

the homicides? Under their fingernails? That was before Helena started."

"I don't have an answer for that yet," I said.

"We'll need it."

"I want to see the evidence."

"Which evidence?" she said.

"The gun, the shirt, the hammer, the video, anything taken from the crime scenes. Can you arrange it?"

"They should comply with the request. If not, I can subpoena it. A lab tech or a detective will bring it to a conference room for us," she said. "But Mackenzie, I reviewed the photographs. It really is your gun, it really is your shirt."

"Let's look anyway."

"Why?" she said.

"Because that's how my work works. No shortcuts. I investigate."

"You wash your own floors," she said, and the lilt had returned in residence to her syllables.

"Bet your ass I do."

"Although, as penance, perhaps I should take a turn scrubbing."

"That is not the penance I require."

"Anything, Mackenzie," she said, "for you."

"You know what would be hot?"

"Mmm. Tell me."

"If you got the evidence this afternoon so I don't have to go back to prison," I said.

"You're right. Acquittals are sexy."

27

Ronnie and I met Detective Archie Hart at the police station after lunch. Hart acted like a man who had his ass handed to him, now eager to play nice.

The charges against me remained. But I bet Green was following up on leads like his life depended on it. Suddenly that girl dancing with Jason Hicks who may or may not have worn a wig was the most important person in Green's life. I wasn't going to tell him yet about my housekeeper, the girl with no hair. Who might wear a wig when she went out dancing.

Ronnie and I waited in the conference room as Archie hauled in black boxes wrapped with yellow tape. He snapped on blue latex gloves and cut the security tape around each box. Later he'd tape them again, to preserve the integrity of his evidence.

"You two don't touch a thing, hear?" he said.

"The video first."

"Video first," he repeated.

He placed a Samsung phone onto the table in front of me. The phone was connected to a portable battery. The screen flickered on, and he used a stylus to open a video and click play.

I recognized Maddie Owens immediately, despite the dimness of her room, and despite her disheveled state. Her skin was unnaturally tight with dermaplaning and whatever else money could buy. Her nose was little and surgically perfected, her eyes large and brown. Time and poor decisions had weathered her during the three years since I'd seen her, especially around the eyes.

She was a crying snotty mess, and she held the phone camera herself, like taking a selfie.

"*Hi. It's me. I... I wanted to make a video, in case... I don't know, in case something bad happens. It won't! But it might. I hope it won't.*" She stopped to sniff and look around her room. "*So here's the truth. I have... I'm having an affair with Mackenzie August. We have been for a while. I don't know how long. He's an investigator in town, and we met years ago. He's famous but he's an awful man. I see that now. I see my mistakes. He's a bad bad man..*" She glanced up again, like something caught her eye. "*I'm getting married soon and Mackenzie found out and...*" She closed her eyes and sobbed for thirty seconds. Grief clenched hard around my heart. Someone was in the room with her, forcing her to say the words. Had to be. When she continued, it was with eyes screwed tight, talking through gasps. "*Mackenzie says... Said he'll kill me. He said he killed two other guys with a hammer last week or something, and now he'll expose our affair, if I don't stop the wedding. He'll humiliate me. Or kill me. So...*" She sniffed. "*Maybe I'll do it myself. Maybe I'll kill myself instead. That way, no one finds out. I don't know... But I'm sorry. I'm really sorry.*"

The video clicked off. The disappearance of her voice was jarring, like she'd died all over again.

"That's rough," I said.

"Rough as hell."

"You're a fool for believing it."

"August, c'mon, man. It's a suicide confession. Right before she shot herself. How're we supposed to not believe that?" said Hart.

Ronnie slid me a handwritten note—*Don't forget, Maddie had a daughter. Brooklyn. No mention of her in the 'suicide note.'*

"Archie, someone was in the room with Maddie. She was glancing around," I said.

Archie shrugged. "Maybe. Could be you."

"I'm forcing her to confess to a crime that implicates me? Hart, be serious. Maddie Owens was a serial adulteress. She boinked anything that moved, and she told the world about it. Now suddenly she's humiliated? Humiliated enough to kill herself? No way. None of this adds up. She didn't even say goodbye to her daughter."

"We're doing our best here, August."

"In fact," I said, "you're not. What about her fiancé?"

"We didn't get much out of him."

"Explain."

"I can't divulge the findings of our investigation—"

"Mr. Hart, this is an open criminal case and I was granted my motion for discovery," said Ronnie. "Answer his question or you'll explain to the judge on speakerphone why you're refusing to cooperate."

Hart rubbed his forehead.

"Yeah," he said. "So. The thing is. Her fiancé wasn't so convinced he was gonna marry the girl. Marry Maddie, I mean."

"He was having second thoughts?" I said.

"Man's name is Tom Romero. And Tom said he hadn't proposed."

"Maddie claimed she was getting married."

"Tom said they talked about it, but it hadn't been a serious thing," said Hart. "He hadn't seen Maddie in over a week. Seemed like a casual thing."

"Maddie claimed she was getting married soon. She said soon."

"I know that, August."

"Is there evidence on her phone she was dating anyone else?" I said.

"No."

"You still think this adds up?" I said.

"The girl had high hopes. No big deal."

"Or it's fictional. Maddie had no good reason to kill herself, so she was fed one, about her upcoming marriage being ruined and her mortification," I said.

"Then why would the girl kill herself, if there was no wedding to ruin?"

"She didn't kill herself. You idiot. The killer forced Maddie to film a suicide note, then shot her with my gun, and then placed the smoking gun into Maddie's dead hand."

"Maybe you did all that," said Hart.

"With my *own* gun? That I left at the scene? After she said it was me? Come ON, Archie!" I shouted.

He nodded and held up his hands. "It's my job to examine all the angles, August. Not all the angles make sense but I gotta ask the questions. And you'll stop shouting at me, you want me to keep playing nice."

"Does Tom Romero have an alibi?" said Ronnie.

"Yes ma'am. He was selling industrial air conditioners

in Lexington all day. Got two eyewitnesses put him there. At least two."

"I want their names," said Ronnie.

"Yes ma'am."

"Show me the gun," I said.

Archie withdrew my .38 Smith & Wesson. He held it by the corners to avoid smudging. Fine fingerprint powder was gathered in the creases of the barrel and grip.

"Looks like mine," I said.

"Serial number's registered to you. Had your prints and Maddie's prints." With a gloved finger, he pointed at the muzzle. "Some of her blood here."

"Did you print the bullets in the chamber?"

His lips pressed together in a line and he shook his head. "No."

Ronnie made a sniffing noise and wrote more on her legal pad. The pad was an orderly world of notes. She was also recording everything on her video phone.

"We will," said Archie. "I'll do it today."

He set the revolver down and picked up the leather holster, dusted with a scrim of white powder.

I nodded. "Mine."

"Figured as much. It was beside Maddie's body."

"It was taken from my nightstand," I said.

"You have proof?"

"I do, but I'm in no hurry to share it. "

"Why's that?" said Archie.

"You guys screw everything up."

He made a wince. "Easy, August. We done?"

"We're looking at everything. Show me the shirt."

"Everything? August, this won't help."

"I follow evidence, Archie. You should try. Show me the shirt."

He opened another box and displayed my shirt, pinching the shoulders. A red Ralph Lauren pullover.

It was mine. I bought it a decade ago at an outlet in Northern Virginia. Seeing it was a shock. I felt strangely humbled and embarrassed and outraged.

The bottom was torn.

Thick shirts don't rip like that, not without help. It hadn't been torn last I'd seen it.

Something...

Something about it aggravated me. When had I last seen it?

Hart draped the shirt across the table and withdrew the second piece, tagged differently for the different crime scene. The small piece matched the torn pullover.

I nodded.

He watched me for a reaction.

I nodded again and I stood and leaned over the shirt, looking closer. Had I worn this recently? I didn't think so. Where had...? Where had I seen this last? My closet?

"You good?" said Archie.

"Shhh." I stepped away from the table. Looking at the floor. Thinking. Remembering. Trying to remember.

Something...

"Mackenzie? What is it?"

"I don't know." I closed my eyes and walked around the conference room table, bumping into chairs with my thighs.

"What's the deal?" said Archie.

"SHHHHH."

That was my red pullover. You know your own clothes when you see them.

And yet...

And yet something wasn't...

"I don't think..."

Eyes still closed. Staring at the shirt.

That shirt hanging in my closet.

That shirt in my laundry.

Me wearing the shirt.

Me folding the shirt.

Me putting the shirt in a box...

"What am I missing?" said Archie.

"ArchieShutUpI'mThinking," I shouted at him.

Me folding the shirt. Me putting the shirt into a cardboard box. Me carrying the box. That shirt in a box.

That shirt in a box...

"I gave that shirt away."

"Gave it away? To Maddie?" said Archie.

"No. I gave it to... Who'd I give it to?"

"Mackenzie, as your attorney, I advise you to work this out later, in private, while the detective isn't listening," said Ronnie. "He doesn't have your best interest—"

I snapped my fingers.

"The Goodwill Store! I donated a box of clothes to the Goodwill. This shirt was in the box."

"How long ago?" said Ronnie.

"Two weeks, maybe three."

"Mackenzie, a box full of your shirts could be transporting pieces of your hair," she said.

"Yes. That explains the DNA."

"Huh?" said the detective.

"I was framed, Archie. Now I have a guess how it was done—my hairs were taken from collars found in a box full of my shirts."

Archie waggled the torn piece of my pullover.

"You think Maddie bought this shirt from Goodwill?"

I bent over Ronnie and kissed her. "Thank you."

"Where are you going?" she said.

"The Goodwill on Melrose. Archie, you want to tag along? See what a real detective does?"

"Slow down, I gotta stash this evidence in the locker. Then I'll go and I don't lose my job."

"That part," I said, "doesn't interest me."

28

The Goodwill Store was a non-profit retail chain that accepted donations and resold them for cheap. The building was new brick with a blue roof and a giant Goodwill logo near the door.

Archie stood out of his unmarked squad car and he said, "My mom used to buy me jeans at Goodwill. And Air Jordans, when they had any."

We walked through the front doors and I told Archie to watch while I talked, and I asked for the manager. The manager was in the back, opening boxes, a woman named Jada. She worked while I talked.

"I donated two boxes of clothing. A red pullover from those boxes was soon after found at a crime scene," I said. "I want to know how it got there."

Jada wiped sweat from her forehead with the back of her wrist. "Yeah, how you gonna do that?"

"I have a few ideas. The best ideas. My suspect is a thin White woman with no hair. If that doesn't sound familiar, I'd like to question your employees about the shirt. We have a photo of it."

"One shirt?" Jada laughed at me. "One damn shirt? We sell a hundred shirts a day. How long ago you talking?"

"I brought it three weeks go."

"So, two thousand shirts since. You want us to remember one shirt in two thousand?" she said.

"Yes please."

"Well don't get your hopes up, big man. You can ask, you want."

"What about a small Caucasian woman with no hair?"

"What about her?" she said.

"Ring any bells?"

"No," said Jada. She took out a sticker gun to mark prices. "No that don't ring any bells. Why don't she have no hair?"

As we spoke, a man arrived, pushing a big squeaky cart of clothing. Bald guy, maybe sixty. He opened one of the enormous washing machines and began shoveling in the load.

"Hey, Arch, how's'a boy," said the bald guy.

"Hey hey, Kenny, how you been," said Archie. "How's your wife, any better?"

"On the mend, but she still mean." The bald guy, Kenny, threw in more clothes and pointed at me. "Arch, you work with this fella?"

"No, Kenny, he ain't police. We, ah, collaborating temporarily."

"Well you just watch your back with him. The guy's a con artist," said Kenny.

Jada took a second look at me. "You a con artist? That right?"

"Would I tell you if I was?" I said.

"This man right here? What'choo talking about, Kenny?" Archie had taken on a more urban dialect since walking in. I wondered if this was his true self, or if Police Station Archie was his true self.

"That man right there." Kenny pointed at me. "I recognize him, big White dude, running a con."

I was stimulated.

"I told Jada about you," said Kenny. "Jada, this is the guy, you remember? Few weeks ago."

"I remember." Jada nodded and began whacking shirt tags with stickers.

"What'd you step in now, August? Maybe you need your lawyer again?"

"I didn't con these people, Archie. How big does the clue need to be before you recognize it?"

"Kenny, tell me the story, huh?" said Archie.

"This man here," said Kenny, "he pulled through the donation line in his car. Popped the trunk and gave me two boxes."

I nodded. "Three weeks ago."

"That's right, three weeks ago. I wrote the man a receipt and he drove off."

I nodded again. "I still have it."

"Then, you know what he did?"

"No, but I'm interested in it," said Archie.

"This man sends his wife through and she picks the boxes back up."

"My wife?" I said.

"Don't act the fool, now. Your wife following you two cars back."

"What'd she do?" said Archie.

"She pulls up and gets out the car and takes the boxes back. Picks the boxes up her own damn self, and she don't say a word until I ask her. She says her husband made a mistake and she still needs that shit. 'Scuse me, that stuff.

She takes both boxes. I say, ma'am, he donated it and I already wrote him the receipt. This is stealing, ma'am, I say. She says, no, she's his wife, and it's her stuff, and she's taking it back, and she drives off."

"My wife was following me?" I said.

"C'mon, you know she was. You get your big tax receipt and you keep all your stuff. Pretty smooth."

"What'd she look like?" said Archie.

"Good-looking blonde woman."

Archie nodded. "Yeah that's her."

"What car was she driving?" I said.

"I don't recall."

"Red Mercedes?"

"Don't think so. That I think I'd remember."

"Jada," I said. "Do you have security cameras monitoring the donation drop-off?"

"Sure do."

"This woman," I said, "I gotta see."

Archie made a grunt. "You and me both."

~

A LARGE LATINO led us into the small, warm security room. He lowered into a swivel chair that threatened collapse.

"Got a Montavue system. Twelve cameras. I keep the last six weeks here." He patted the big black box. "Six terabytes. After a month, film gets deleted."

"Go to..." I checked my phone's calendar. "The last Friday in March."

The large Latino breathed and rattled through his nose, and he used a mouse to select the date. Archie and I watched over his shoulder.

"Sometime in the early afternoon," I said.

He nodded and wheezed and brought up two cameras aimed at the drop-off. The video clarity was excellent—bright light and the world looked crisp and blue. He began fast-forwarding at noon.

"There's Kenny." Archie pointed at the screen. The day had been chilly and Kenny wore a toboggan. I remembered him now.

He slowed the video anytime a car appeared, which happened once every three or four minutes.

I arrived at 1:30pm.

"There," I said. "That's my Honda."

He tapped a button and the video returned to normal speed.

Archie leaned forward to watch. "Gonna need a copy of this."

The large guy said, "Uh huh."

On screen, I popped the trunk and handed two big cardboard boxes to Kenny. He made small talk, his breath clouding, and wrote me a receipt and I motored away.

I wrinkled my nose. "Need to straighten my shoulders some."

A truck drove into view. Kenny took a bike off the truck bed. The driver declined the receipt and drove off.

Another car braked quickly behind. Not a red Mercedes. A Hyundai Sonata. I made a note of the plate.

A blonde woman stood out of the car. She wore jeans and a windbreaker.

"There," said Archie. "It's her."

"That's not my wife."

"Blonde." Archie squinted and leaned closer to the screen.

"The hair's too short. And Ronnie would die before she wore a windbreaker," I said.

The woman walked directly to the boxes and picked up one of mine while Kenny watched, befuddled. She turned and strode back to her car.

I saw her face.

My stomach tightened.

"*Ooh.*"

The Latino paused the video. Archie squinted at it.

The woman frozen on screen looked thirty-ish. Short. Blonde hair to her chin. She'd be cute if her face wasn't set in a mask of anger. She looked furious.

"That ain't your wife," said Archie.

I knew the face. It took me a second, but I placed her. I knew her and I knew her name. Her first name at least.

"Oh man," I said.

"What?"

I took a photo of the woman on screen with my phone.

"Oh man," I said again.

"What's the deal?"

"Archie, I gotta run."

"Bullshit you do."

"I'll fill you in soon," I said. "I got a lot of work to do."

"August, this is a homicide investigation! You're charged with murder. Who is that woman?"

"Sorry, Arch." I grinned. "I can't divulge my investigative findings. You understand."

29

Here's the thing about big reveals—they're rare.

I've had a few in my career, where I gather invested parties and let the cat out of the bag, and everyone understands all at once. Sometimes the guilty party is present, which makes for high drama. Sherlock Holmes might've invented the big reveal, which was subsequently picked up by Hercule Poirot? I didn't know, but I was grateful for the idea.

Anyway, perfect big reveals were rare and tonight wouldn't be one. But it'd be good nonetheless. I was a showman.

I ordered Chinese food and Beck offered to pick it up on her way in, eager to attend because I'd spread a rumor that tonight I'd explain much of the crime. We sat at the table and circulated containers of General Tso's chicken and drunken noodles and fried rice and sushi, and each person piled his or her own plate to overflowing. Laughter and soy sauce flowed.

I'd finished half my Gold Leaf Lager when someone knocked. I answered and let Marcus Morgan into our soiree. A little out of place, he was dressed better than us. And he was somber. And wore sunglasses indoors. And he was Black, and we weren't.

"Everyone, you know Marcus," I said. "He's never done anything illegal."

"Sounds boring to me," said Stackhouse, and a place was made for him.

He sat next to Noelle Beck and smiled down at her. "I assume you're an officer of the law, too."

"National Security Agency, on loan to the marshals," said Noelle, who looked like a twelve-year-old in comparison. "Noelle Beck."

"Kinda little," he said.

"Manny won't let me eat more."

"Me either," I said.

Marcus and Manny had a long and complicated relationship that involved no small amount of looking the other way for the sake of maintaining order. Tonight would be no different.

"You tell people what to eat," said Marcus.

Manny made a scoff. "Of course. We let insane people make decisions? They'd be dipping french fries into milk shakes without me."

"White people crazy," said Marcus.

Ronnie made a plate of sushi for Marcus and he thanked her, and I stood and said, "Let's begin."

"Finally," said Timothy August.

"I'm so excited," said Noelle.

Kix was nodding off in his high chair next to Ronnie and he mumbled something about staying up late with the adults.

"I know most," I said. "But not all. Some will be

conjecture, and the guilty party is not among us. That's still to be resolved."

"Ay, just tell us who did it," said Manny.

"I require a long-suffering audience."

"Don't listen to Manny," said Ronnie. "You have my attention all night."

"Our story begins with Danil Turgenev. He was a Russian accountant in Newark, who I believe specialized in tax fraud on behalf of his countrymen. At some point last year, his fortunes changed and he was cast into disfavor. Maybe he owed the Russian Brotherhood money and he couldn't pay, maybe he stole from a casino in Brooklyn, maybe he slept with the wrong woman, who knows. The point is, he got the hell out of Brooklyn in a hurry and he started life anew, in Roanoke, Virginia. Danil changed his name to Donald Torres, procured new identification, and carved a living out of the stock market, trading stocks. Judging by his travel itinerary, he'd finally earned enough to move to Beirut.

"Unfortunately for Danil, he didn't run fast enough. A hitman for the Russians found him here. But the hitman didn't just find Danil. The hitman found me too."

"Question." Manny raised his hand. "This hitman, he know you were here before he took the job?"

"Good question, Manny."

"*Gracias.*"

"I don't know the answer. My guess is, it was a coincidence. A good coincidence for the hitman, a bad one for me. And I'll drop a hint here—the hitman is not a man. The hitman is a woman," I said. "Hereafter referred to as an assassin, because hitwoman isn't a word."

Timothy August muttered, "I have a bad feeling about where this is headed."

"The assassin arrives in Roanoke. Before she carries out her hit on the Russian accountant, she either intentionally locates her old pal Mackenzie August, or she accidentally discovers I'm here, probably from one of the absurd online articles written about me. She cannot let this opportunity pass. After all, she has reason to hate me, and also reason to hate Ronnie."

Noelle Beck raised her hand now. "You two know her? How?"

"Why does she hate me?" said Ronnie. "I'm adorable."

"This is fabulous," said Stackhouse. "Just fabulous."

Timothy made a *not-so-sure* grimace. "Assuming it ends well."

"To continue," I said. "The assassin gets an idea. What if she carries out her hit, *and* she pins it on me? Revenge, after all, is a dish best served cold. The assassin sees her opportunity three weeks ago, as she's following me around town. I deliver a box of clothing to the Goodwill. Inspiration strikes, and she scoops up my belongings, providing her with my DNA, taken from my shirts. Hair and flakes of skin."

"You should use a better shampoo," said Manny. "What have I been telling you."

"Now she's ready. The assassin goes to the home of Donald Torres and kills him with a hammer. She's a pro. She leaves no evidence, other than my hair and skin, which she carefully plants under Donald's fingernails. She absconds. And she waits.

"However. A few days go by, and the dead body hasn't been discovered yet. She's getting itchy. She needs another victim. So she goes to a club downtown and seduces Jason Hicks, local single man. She puts on a brown wig and she talks to him, finds out where he lives, finds out he's single, finds out he has a dog but the dog is friendly, and just when Jason thinks everything is going great, she dumps him. She can't be seen leaving with the victim, after all. She's too good. Instead, she's waiting inside Jason's house when he returns. Probably behind his bedroom door. Jason walks in, and *pow*." I clapped my hands and my audience flinched. "Jason dies by the same hammer. More evidence is planted. And here she also leaves a piece of my shirt, meaning she's got a third victim in mind already."

"She's a calculating bitch, isn't she," said Stackhouse. She and Timothy were holding hands.

"I don't know if the assassin shaved her head, or if she used a prosthetic bald cap to pretend she was cancerous—"

"Dammit," said Timothy. "I knew it. I knew this would fall on Helena. And on me."

"It's okay, babe. She fooled all of us."

"Not me and Mack," said Manny. "Honorable Americans."

"The assassin shaves her head, or dons the cap, waits until Ronnie and I are gone for the day, and knocks on the door. She has a list of fake references and a sob story. Look at her head, after all. She lost her hair to the cancer and she has no money and—"

"I get it! I screwed up and I feel awful about it. Move along," said Timothy.

"Inside our home she's able to collect more DNA from our marital bed. Perhaps she was unable to, her first trip, which is why she returned for a second. While in my bedroom, she strikes gold—my revolver inside the nightstand," I said.

"I have another question, if that's okay?" Noelle raised her hand again. "Why wouldn't the assassin just kill you?"

"What a great question. Bonus points for you," I said.

"Why's she get bonus points? We all thinking it," said Marcus.

"She was brave enough to ask. To answer, I have several guesses. One, she's not a shooter. Most of her work involves poison, which she might've resorted to if I hadn't been arrested. Two, if she got close to me, I'd recognize her. Three, she hates Ronnie too, not just me. Four, she knows about Manny and that concerns her. Five, I'm well-known in her world and killing me wouldn't be a popular decision. Instead, she arranged it so I would be hoisted by my own petard."

"What," said Manny, "in the absolute hell does—"

"After having total autonomy in our house twice, she's armed with more DNA and my gun. She's ready for her third victim."

"How'd she decide on poor Maddie Owens?" asked Stackhouse.

"Please raise your hand first."

"Babe, I'll pour this wine onto your perfect floor. Don't think I won't," she said.

"I figured it out today, after a Google search. Maddie Owens had been bragging in the comments section of a recent article written about me. She claimed to have had an affair with me a few years ago, and she even signed her name. It's a lie that got her killed, because the assassin saw it and tracked her down. Maddie's comment made the fake suicide look much more realistic."

"Why did the assassin not kill Maddie with a hammer?" said Timothy. "Lord, what a ghastly question."

"Because the detectives hadn't arrested me. She reasoned they didn't have enough evidence yet, and she needed more. A confession would do nicely. She entered

Maddie's home and forced her to record a fake confession, probably promising to leave immediately after, with Maddie unharmed. Maddie was terrified, which made the video look better. Video completed, she shot Maddie in the head, slipped my revolver into her hand, deposited my shirt under the bed, and left. That was Wednesday. I was arrested Friday, and I bet you a dozen donuts that she was long gone by Saturday. I was in jail. Ronnie had learned her husband was a philanderer. Revenge served. Russian dead. Mission accomplished."

Ronnie was absently stroking Kix's hair. He was asleep. She said, "She's thorough."

"She is. It would've worked if you hadn't been able to spring me on bail, and if the detectives hadn't botched so much of their job, and if she hadn't been caught on camera, and if I wasn't so damn impressive," I said.

Manny tapped the table a few times, hard. "Great story, *amigo*. Now tell us who it is."

"Your clues are, she's a hitman who works in the underworld. She works with poisons. She's blonde. She doesn't like me or Ronnie."

"Ooooh." Ronnie's eyes, far-off, snapped into focus on me. "I know. I know!"

"*Who*?" Stackhouse said.

"What's-her-name, the girl from Italy."

I set my phone on the table so everyone could see the photograph from Goodwill. The blonde carrying my cardboard box.

"Everyone, meet Meg."

Timothy leaned toward it and said, "That's Helena! With hair."

"Who is Meg?" said Noelle Beck. "What about Italy?"

"*Nothing* about Italy," said Manny. "Don't be nosey, Beck."

"Meg is a physician who accepted employment with Darren Robbins to pay off her mountain of school debt, the only job she could land after multiple indiscretions. She abducted me three years ago. Took me right out of my office with a medicinal cocktail, and I was whisked off to Naples. She was my handler, keeping me sedated with drugs. She tried to kill me at the end, but Ronnie intervened. She shot at Meg and missed."

"Twice, didn't I? I fired two or three times," said Ronnie.

"Yes. She was begging for her life, but you kept shooting. And missing."

Manny snorted. "Missing."

"I called her a bitch too. I told her to run away and never come back," said Ronnie. "No wonder she's angry."

Marcus spoke for the first time in several minutes. "I looked her up. Girl goes by Domino now. Works for a man named Lorenzo Puddu, who takes high-priced contracts and sends killers around the world. Puddu says Domino drove to Charlotte Saturday and caught a flight to Bermuda, where she's at right this minute."

"You know Lorenzo Puddu?" said Timothy.

"No. But I know people who know shit. They didn't know Turgenev, but they know Domino."

"So we call Bermuda and have her picked up?" said Noelle.

"I'm on a plane tomorrow," I said. "It's better I do it, rather than the Bermuda Service. She's good and I don't trust anybody else, based on recent police behavior."

"Mackenzie," said Ronnie, "you're wearing an ankle

monitor. Judge Newman was sweet on you but you'll be arrested all over again if you fly to Bermuda."

"I've written a strongly worded apology, to be sent via email as the plane lifts off," I said.

"I'll go too," said Manny. "You go in the company of a marshal, and you help apprehend a criminal, maybe you don't go tittup."

"That's not how the word works."

"I don't care. Gonna keep using it, *amigo*. What it means is, maybe the judge be cool with you."

"Violations of parole are not excused by apologies or the proximity of a deputy marshal." Ronnie smiled at my simplicity. "But we'll get the charges reduced to something inconsequential. You have an excellent lawyer on retainer and she's in love with you."

30

That night I brushed my teeth twice and flossed and gargled with minty Scope. I'd doubled my oral scrubbing since prison, like the bad coffee remained imbedded in my enamel. I took a moment to survey the man in the mirror.

A haircut was called for soon. Flecks of gray were creeping into the brown thatch, like an old roof. More so in the scruff of my chin and jaw, but I liked it. I was down twenty pounds from my heyday in Los Angeles, wearing muscles like ballistic armor, but now my knees creaked on the stairs. I was still big—did I need to lose more? Were my eyes puffy? Did these dark circles qualify as bags? My eyebrows didn't used to require maintenance but they were unruly now, and I was weekly plucking hair out of my ear. That was something no one prepared you for. Ear hair. Seemed contrary to me, that the closer one came to being a gentleman, the harder one had to work to look it.

"Should I grow a beard," I asked myself.

"To hide the wrinkles? Maybe," replied Manny. "If you won't use night cream."

He was in the hallway, arms crossed, leaning against the wall next to my bedroom. He was nude except for the leather bracelet his nephew made and a tight pair of boxers, displaying a body of lean muscle, scar tissue, and tattoos. I joined.

"I don't have wrinkles. I have laugh lines."

"You don't laugh, *señor*."

"Laughing's for sissies," I said. "But I produce the lines anyway."

"Ay. Before we go to Bermuda. We need to talk about the hitman."

"Meg," I said.

"She's a problem."

"I know."

"Even when we bring her in, and show the Goodwill photo to the dumbass detectives, and explain she was pretending to be a housekeeper, there's nothing to charge her with murder. *Señorita* was too good," said Manny.

"It'll be enough to get my charges dropped. And when she's printed and her face is scanned, it'll ring databases for the FBI or CIA or DEA or somebody."

"That's the problem."

"She knows too much," I said.

"Way too much. I watch this happen a lot. She'll turn state's evidence. She's gonna tell the FBI about you and Ronnie and Darren What's-his-name, and Marcus Morgan, and Naples, and the District Kings. All that mafia garbage. Then she'll tell the CIA about Lorenzo Puddu and the Russians. Girl will sing to save her ass."

"I thought this through. I don't know how exposed Ronnie and I are, though."

"Makes me nervous, *amigo*. You're tied to the Kings in a lot of ways. Your life could get weird fast. Whole branches of government dedicated to organized crime and they all gonna wanna squeeze you," he said.

"The most important thing is getting the charges dropped. To do that, I need her. Once I have her, I'll think through the rest."

The door to my bedroom opened.

Ronnie said, "I overheard someone wants to squeeze Mackenzie. Someone other than me."

She wore only a short red baby doll chemise by La Perla. The silk-satin hid nothing and highlighted everything, and Manny and I were struck mute.

"Who else wants to squeeze you?" she said.

"There is no one else."

She took my hand. "Come to bed."

Manny cleared his throat. "I'll get my pillow."

"You're not invited, Manny."

"I'll sleep in the hallway and listen."

"Better yet, go knock on Noelle's door," said Ronnie.

"Noelle who?"

"Don't be obtuse. You know you think about her. I see you," she said.

Manny gave her a deadly glower. "*Mujer*, I don't know what you're talking about."

"Are you wearing oil in your hair?" I said. "To sleep?"

"Argan and obviously. When's the last time you saw me with a bad hair day? *Buenas noches*." He went into his room and shut the door hard.

Ronnie took my other hand. "Husband."

"Your lingerie might kill him."

"Manny can have any woman in the city. He abstains." She tugged me into our bedroom. "Well. Any woman except yours," she said.

"My woman."

"Your woman. For always."

31

Manny Martinez had a well-known and celebrated career as a Deputy US Marshal. However, he also worked as a clandestine federal operative doing Captain America things, but he didn't share much about it and I didn't ask much. For this position, he was provided wide autonomy and a credit card with no limit, and he used it to book first-class tickets and a room at the St. Regis Bermuda Resort, where Meg the assassin stayed.

On the flight over, the stewardess grew so nervous around him that she spilled cranberry juice on the couple across the aisle. Manny didn't notice or didn't care, too bent on arguing that arresting Meg wasn't wise. That Ronnie was a good lawyer and I'd never be convicted, even without Meg, and we should do that instead.

"She hurt Ronnie," was my final answer. "She hurt my marriage."

"Not anymore."

"She might try again," I said.

"Marcus can talk to Lorenzo, her handler. Say you're off limits."

"She hurt Ronnie."

"She's gonna cause trouble. For everybody," said Manny. "All the mafia shit she knows?"

"She hurt Ronnie."

"*Ay, eres un tonto obstinado.*" He drained his mimosa, frustrated, and the stewardess hurried to refill the flute.

~

MARCUS' intel was pinpoint accurate.

We located Meg the assassin on Saint Catherine's Beach, at the northern tip of Bermuda. A quiet place, backed by green grass and palm trees, and fronted by a coral sea stretching to the eternal horizon. The sun hung in the sky, two in the afternoon, and a breeze mustered enough to toss strands of her blonde hair.

Her blonde hair. A pixie cut, like I'd seen Charlize Theron wear. At least six months of growth.

Manny and I took weathered Adirondack chairs on the grass, fifty yards behind the beach, and surveyed the scene behind our sunglasses. Meg, also known as Domino, reclined on a cushioned beach chair next to a man too old and fat to have earned her though legitimate means, their backs to us.

"She's not bald," I said.

Manny grunted. He wore a white linen shirt and wayfarer glasses and a straw Panama hat and he looked like he owned all of paradise.

"You said she was bald," I said.

"She fooled me."

"You said her hair was growing back."

"She wore one of those red handkerchiefs with the bald wig and I saw some blonde hair, and I thought... *Ay caramba*, I don't explain myself to you, with your baseball cap," he said.

"What's wrong with my baseball cap?"

"You're in Bermuda, that's what."

We ordered Mai Tais and watched and waited and soaked the equatorial sunlight.

As far as we could see, Meg and the man she was with had one bodyguard, a burly guy wearing a polo shirt, sitting closer to the resort. He took note of us soon after our arrival, and Manny threw him a nod, but the bodyguard didn't reply, which was, I thought, hurtful.

Meg and the man read on the beach for the next two hours, wading into the crystal water once. She was recuperating from the exhaustion of framing me for murder.

"It's not too late," said Manny. "We find some way to solve this without the mess."

"I solve messes for a living."

"She knows too much. You gone be a bus driver now. Could hurt Ronnie's career too."

"Let's go," I said.

We returned to St. Regis and waited in ambush.

~

MEG and the man returned to their suite before dinner. The door beeped and opened, and they stepped into their entryway. The man was chattering in Italian, a deep voice, and I couldn't follow it. Manny and I stood in the sunshine on their balcony, watching through the open doors.

Meg closed the door. She was as I remembered—smallish, trim, cute if she didn't wear disgust as her natural visage. She took off her sunglasses and set them on the bamboo sideboard, and she shook out her hair, and that's when she saw us.

"Oh," said Meg. "*Oh!* Lorenzo!"

Lorenzo Puddu was the man escorting her. An Italian who'd lost his hair except above the ears. His shirt was unbuttoned and his tanned smooth stomach protruded from it. Some Italian word I couldn't read was tattooed across his chest. A powerful figure in the underworld.

"Hm?" He saw us and his eyes lighted. "Oh, it is them!"

"It's them, Lorenzo!" She grabbed the man's arm. "*Sono loro! Gli, ah... assassini!*"

"You came!" Lorenzo held out his hands and smiled. "Signore Marcus, he said you would! Come in! *Per favore.* I am happy to meet you!"

I stepped inside and Manny followed.

Lorenzo took my hand in both of his.

"You! You I know! I was in Naples, of course. I watched you fight!" He raised up his arms and flexed muscles. "The American! The Yankee! *Campione della Gabbia Cremisi!*"

"I bet I cost you money," I said.

"*Milioni!* I bet on Il Principe, of course. But the Italians, we still love you. For the fight!"

Meg couldn't get enough air.

"Lorenzo, no... This is... These men can't be here," she said. She licked her lips and clutched at her coverup. She was thinner than when I'd last seen her. No longer a well-fed medical student, but a lean professional killer. If stereotypes held true, she turned to narcotics to support herself through the emotional tolls, another reason she was too thin.

"Yes I know." Lorenzo turned from us to eye her, and he lost his warmth. "I was told, *amore*. I was told what you did."

"I... I did as I was ordered. Danil, he is dead," she said.

"I know. I know you killed Danil Turgenev," said Lorenzo.

"Yes."

"But you went too far. *Hai fatto un errore*. Didn't you, Domino," he said.

"I... He..."

"Meg and I are old friends. Did she tell you?" I said.

"*Sì*. She did. That is why she was hired, after Naples." He grinned. "Tell me, *prego*. Do you still have the tattoo?"

I nodded.

"I do."

"*Lo sapevo*! I will tell my *amici* about this!"

"Lorenzo..." said Meg. "I don't understand. Mackenzie is supposed to be in prison. How did they find... How did you know?"

Lorenzo made a wave of his hand and stepped heavily to the bar. He poured himself rum. "You did not fulfill the contract, Domino."

"I did!"

He pointed at her and glared, and it was a good glare.

Lorenzo, scary guy.

"You made it a heart attack?"

"I..." she said.

"No. You used a..." He snapped his fingers a couple times.

"Hammer," said Manny.

"Hammer! You used a hammer. You killed more people and you did it like..." He pointed at me now, with the hand holding the glass. "...like he did it. Like the Yankee did it."

"She framed me," I said.

"Yes! Framed. You framed the American King! Marcus, a good man in America, he told me about it."

"Lorenzo. I didn't know it would upset you." Meg was apologizing now, like a lover would. "I would never have..."

"You two," said Manny. "You're together?"

"Yes, I love him," said Meg.

"Bah." Lorenzo waved it away. "She is good. She is very good, yes? She says she loves me now, but... She does not. She pretends it. She *scopa* any man."

"Lorenzo! *No*!" Meg had been edging toward the bedroom door. Without seeming to hurry, Manny moved there first. Blocking the doorway and smiling like it'd been innocent. "They'll kill me!" she said.

"I'm not killing you," I said. "I need you to tell the detectives I'm innocent. I dislike prison."

"I can't! They'll never let me out. Lorenzo, you'll never see me again! *Per favore, mia cara, ti amo*." She turned from Manny to the big man, pleading.

"*Abbiamo finito*. American King, you can take her. Take the bitch away."

"*What!*"

"Please," he said. "Tell the Americans, Lorenzo, he does good work. He is honest. And he is sorry about this..." He indicated Meg like she was a messy pile of laundry.

Manny caught her wrists and cuffed the first, one quick motion.

Meg screamed, "No! You pig! *Maledetto maiale!*" She jumped at Lorenzo but Manny had her and she was yanked backward. Her second wrist was cuffed to the first. "I'll kill you all! *Ti ucciderò*!"

An urgent knock at the door.

Lorenzo answered it and spoke to the bodyguard, told him everything was as it should be. The guy peered over Lorenzo's shoulder, verifying. Nodded once and left.

Lorenzo spread out his hands to us again, smiling, like Meg wasn't weeping in the hands of her captor.

"You two. Take her to prison and come back! We talk fighting. We talk Naples!"

"Lorenzo, you have fonder memories of it than I do," I said.

"*Sì, haha*! The Americans, they haven't been welcomed back! You burned it down! Not until this year, I am told, can you return. But you? The Yankee! You could return as a king!" He waved his hands enough to spill his rum.

"I am returning," I said. "Home, where I'm a dad. And that's enough."

Manny made a shrug.

"Doesn't sound as much fun," he said.

"You are famous in Naples! In the world! You killed all the men you fought."

"In fact, I didn't," I said, and I slipped the phone from my shirt pocket, where it'd been recording the encounter. "Probably have to delete that part, huh."

Meg groaned and sagged, only held up by Manny's strong hands on her arms.

32

In our suite, Meg was talkative and outraged. She implicated Lorenzo and other men I didn't know, blaming me and Manny for her disastrous life after the tournament, accusing us of burning down a hotel in Naples, Italy, and killing scores of men. She raged and spit, declaring she knew my wife was a prostitute. That she knew I worked in the underworld. That I should be incarcerated the rest of my life, and so should my whore of a wife. That if I didn't release her, powerful men would kill me. That she would sell her story to HBO. She admitted some things I knew, and some things I didn't, and promised if we didn't let her go she'd tell the whole world, and I recorded it.

She was armed to the teeth with information the CIA and FBI would gobble up. We listened for an hour. Then Manny cuffed her to the bed and we shut the door against her shouting.

Manny shook his head. "Mack."

"I know."

"She's gonna take you down with her."

"I know. But still. I'll figure it out."

Manny walked to the hotel's restaurant to get us dinner while I transferred the long videos from my phone to my MacBook. Using the editing software, I chopped out sections of our evening.

"I was told, amore. I was told what you did."

"I… I did as I was ordered. Danil, he is dead."

"I know. I know you killed Danil Turgenev."

"Yes."

"But you went too far."

And later…

"You did not fulfill the contract, Domino."

"I did!"

"You made it a heart attack?"

"I…"

"No. You used a…"

"Hammer."

"Hammer! You used a hammer. You killed more people and you did it like… Like he did it. Like the Yankee did it."

"She framed me."

"Yes! Framed. You framed the American King! Marcus, an important man in America, he told me about it."

"Lorenzo. I didn't know it would upset you. I would never have…"

Plus additional implications later, when she fumed and swore at us. Not all of it could be used, though, not without destroying the lives of Marcus and Ronnie.

Meg seemed less sane than three years ago. Years of criminal work, of executions, had cracked her open and filled her with madness.

But I had enough. The charges would be dropped. No more squeeze dogs for me.

I sent the short video clips to Ronnie and Stackhouse, and wondered if the rest should be destroyed or not. It felt like my hands were burning, holding molten rocks. Molten rocks that might burn my house down when they got loose.

~

MANNY RETURNED AN HOUR LATER, pushing a cart laden with fish chowder and rum cake and cocktails.

"Local specialities," he said.

Sitting at the couch, feet up, watching ESPN, I took a bowl of chowder, aromatic and spicy like gumbo, and thanked him. The day had been long, the food taking on greater importance.

He tried a bite too. Declared it not as good Puerto Rican Sancocho, but still edible. He drained half his rum swizzle.

"She awake?" he said.

"She quit shouting twenty minutes ago."

"You think we got enough testimony that your charges will be dropped."

"Ronnie viewed the clips and said we have more than enough. We're set."

"*Bien*. Then I'll feed her."

Meg's room was directly behind my position on the couch and Manny walked into it with a tray of food.

I tried the swizzle. Tasted like fresh fruit and top shelf liquor.

"This cocktail," I called, "might be worth the return trip to Naples."

—CRACK—

A gunshot. Louder for the surprise, and my ears rang.

I jumped up, sloshing the drink.

"Manny!"

I pulled the Kimber 1911 from my side holster. Jumping the coffee table.

"Ay!" he shouted.

"Manny!"

"I'm good!"

My heart thumped hard against my ribs. I ran at Meg's room as he stepped out of it, holding her tray of food.

"*Está bien. Estoy bien.*"

"What happened?"

"Meg. *Señorita*'s dead," said Manny.

"She's dead."

"Gunshot wound to the head. A revolver in her hand."

I believed him. I believed him, but still I cautiously peeked around the doorway, like she might shoot at me, my pulse and the gunshot hurting my brain. Singed gunpowder in my nostrils.

Meg's left wrist was still cuffed to the headboard. A spatter of red gore was glowing dark on the lamp. In her right hand I saw a gun. A cheap little revolver. I stepped close enough to inspect her corpse. The scene looked like wine had spilled across the white comforter.

Meg the assassin would no longer be a problem.

33

Manny called his supervisor within the FBI.

He told her he was in Bermuda, where he'd arrested a dangerous woman in the underworld, an assassin who would've been an embarrassment to a lot of people. He'd cuffed the assassin but she had procured a revolver and killed herself. Now what?

He listened a few minutes and hung up.

We reserved a second room at the St. Regis and transferred into it. Members of his task force within the FBI would arrive soon and *clean* our previous hotel suite. Would handle the corpse.

I ordered us additional rum cake and swizzles. Not because I felt festive. Less celebratory, more medicinal. I remained jumpy.

We sat on the balcony and watched the moon rise over the dark Atlantic. The warm breeze on my face could be a waft from Morocco on the coast of Africa. Before us, the great body of water, connected to the other great bodies around the globe, looked to be heaving south, and us an immoveable speck. What was south? Nothing? Nothing until Brazil? A sobering notion, our infinitesimal insignificance awash in the eternal Earthen floods. A view best enjoyed with a friend and a cocktail.

There was much I wanted to ask Manny about what happened when he walked into Meg's room. About the sudden appearance of the revolver. About his concern for me and Ronnie.

But I already knew the answers.

Manny was a man who didn't let others wash his floors. Who cleaned up messes without trusting to specialists. Who would swim the Atlantic for a friend, would do anything for a friend.

So I said, "Meg died after recording a confession. She died in bed, shot in the temple with a revolver. She died holding the gun. Sounds a lot like the death of Maddie Owens."

"Poetic, *sí*?"

"And just," I said.

"And the señorita's secrets die with her. Better for everyone."

I drank rum, the ice tinkling in the glass.

"Better for everyone except Detective Green," I said.

"His primary suspect, you, got a girl to confess but then she died. You think he'll cause problems?"

I grinned.

"No. He won't."

34

Detective Green lived in a townhouse near the airport, off Dent Road. A small quiet community that was probably glad to have a cop.

The day after Manny and I flew back, I knocked on Green's door after the sun went down. He opened it and I could see into his place—he'd been sitting on the couch watching a movie. He wore Nike shorts and a Virginia Tech T-shirt.

"Ah Christ, August."

"C'mon out, Green."

He held up his hands. "I'm counseling the Commonwealth to drop the charges and I even left you a voicemail, apologizing. What else do you want?"

"Coming out? Or am I coming in?" I was in a mean mood.

"That's it? We're going to fight each other like kids after school?"

"I earned this."

"Shit." He stepped outside and pointed at his car. "See

that, August? That's a detective's cruiser. You think you can assault an officer? You just got out of Roanoke City Jail, you want back in?"

"I told you this was gonna happen. You should've been practicing." I walked to the dark yard beside his townhouse.

"You hit me, it's a felony."

"You charged me with homicides you know I didn't commit. You did your job poorly and it hurt my family. A felony is worth it."

"I thought you were an upstanding guy!" he said. "Now this? Now you're this guy? Now you're a prick?"

I took off my black North Face and threw it in the grass. The motion hurt my ribs a little. I wore a T-shirt too. This part of his neighborhood was unlit. No one would see us.

"I'd hit me first, I was you, Green."

"For Christ's sake. Grow up! I'm a Roanoke City Detective!" He was shouting now. Jumpy and scared. "I was doing my job! I'm not going to hit you."

"Then I'll use you as a heavy bag," I said.

He did hit me, the liar. It was good, a snap from the shoulder instead of a big windup. His left hand, which I heard crack on impact, caught me in the cheek. He followed with a right cross but I moved and it scraped my forehead.

I put a right into his stomach and he doubled over, groaning. A big right, lots of muscle behind it.

I pushed him back up and held him with my left.

Hit him another right. In the teeth, and his lip split and he fell.

He didn't attempt getting up.

I wasn't even panting.

"That's all?"

"Fuck you, August. You busted my mouth." He spit into the grass. "You're going back to jail, and not even your fairy godmother Stackhouse can rescue you."

I kicked him in the stomach. Like I had as a boy playing kickball. He groaned again, a coughing gagging sound, and I knew it was a sick feeling, and he'd be sore for days.

I crouched next to him and set my phone on the ground. The bright screen was dazzling in the darkness. Meg the assassin named Domino was sitting on her bed.

I pressed play and the video resumed, Meg in mid-chatter.

"This will blow up in your face, you sonsofbitches. I swear to God it will! I know so much about you. I know so much, SO FUCKING MUCH. If you don't release me, your career is over. Are you listening? You can quit smiling, because it will be OVER. I'll tell them everything. Your wife will lose her bar card, your fucking child will be raised by some grandparent or aunt or something. Even Detective Green's going down, if you don't release me. Did you think about that? Maybe he'll decide to save his own career and he'll shoot you?"

On screen, I said, *"When you're spilling your guts to the FBI, what will you tell them about Green?"*

"I'll ruin every life I can, Mackenzie. Believe me. Believe me. Every. Life."

"You can't ruin Green's."

"Of course I can! I have the texts to prove it!"

"What texts, Meg?"

"You think he found Maddie by himself? You think he knew where to find the hammer? I'll admit it, I'm a vengeful bitch. I'll cut him down too."

"You and Green," I said.

"Me and Green."

"You had an affair?"

"I did what I had to do."

"How did you know him?" I said.

Meg threw back her head and laughed.

"Oh my GOD. You two don't know anything. It's almost adorable. Green works for Doyle.

"Listen. I did whatever I had to do. I have been for years. And I'll do whatever I have to, now. Trust me, Mackenzie. You don't want to do this. Here's a better idea—I'll record a confession and you let me go, and you'll never hear from me again."

I hit pause.

Sudden loud silence in the grass. Green was on his stomach, face down.

"How about that, Green," I said.

"Yeah."

"How'd you know to check Maddie's apartment for a body, Green?"

He was drooling spit and blood into the grass.

I said, "And who's Doyle?"

"You don't know him?"

"I don't."

"Better for you if it stays that way, August."

"You were having an affair with the person who killed Torres and Hicks and Maddie. And you blamed it on me."

"Listen, August..." He shook his head and sighed into the ground. "August, I'm sorry about it. I didn't know she was... It was after the investigation started that I met her, and I didn't know who she was until it was too late. It was a one-time thing, and... And I swear to God, I didn't know she'd done it. At the beginning, I truly thought it was you, honest."

"My wife spent a miserable weekend wondering if I had an affair with Maddie."

"I'm *sorry*. What else do you want me to say?"

"The truth."

"The truth," said Green. "She picked me up. We had a great night. Next day, she says I'm gonna find another body. And I need to put you away for good. I fought her on it, but she said I should talk to Doyle, and Doyle said I had to do it."

"I thought she worked for Puddu."

"I don't know a Puddu. I know a Doyle. She probably worked for both. Like me, I'm a cop but I do some work for Doyle on the side."

"Does Archie?"

He snorted and then grunted like the snort hurt.

"No. Archie's too straight. Anyway. Like she told me I would, I found Maddie dead with the video about you. I feel bad about all this shit. Okay? But it's done. It's over. I apologized. My boss kicked my ass. You're in the clear and that girl's dead, it's *over*."

I picked up my phone and stood. My right hand stung, still not fully healed from the boxing match with Mr. Clean. And tomorrow my cheek would be swollen. I wanted to keep hitting him. Break some bones and declare something like—*That's for my wife!*

Maybe another time.

"I'm keeping the video, Green. And one day, when I care more about Doyle, you're gonna tell me," I said.

He remained quiet in the grass, on his face and cradling his stomach.

"Make this whole thing go away, Green."

"I am. I will. You have my word."

"Call the parents of Jason Hicks and apologize for being an incompetent asshat," I said.

"Yeah sure thing."

"And send my wife some flowers." I turned for my car, sneakers squeaking in the grass, then crunching on gravel.

"Up yours, August."

"You probably couldn't even get that right."

~

I STAYED in my car half an hour, long after Green limped inside his townhouse.

It would be tricky for him. He'd arrested the wrong guy and he had some 'splaining to do. To his boss. To Judge Newman. To Doyle. Green was lead investigator on two homicides, and now his primary suspect was a woman who killed herself in Bermuda, and he was telling everyone the case could be closed. Tricky indeed.

The way he talked about Doyle made me nervous. I was sick of underworld entanglements. I blew a sigh at my window and it fogged.

Ronnie texted.

>> **Darling husband. Mackenzie.**

>> **Please pick up a bottle of champagne on your way home? I need to numb myself.**

>> **Manny brought home a board game called Risk and is demanding we play.**

"Jiminy Christmas," I said. "We need something stronger than champagne."

What was worse? Game night, or fighting Mr. Clean? They held an equivalency of violence. At least tonight I'd get to sleep in the same room as a cute girl. And probably a Manny.

I started the car.

THE END

Dear Reader,

WOULD you like an insight into the fascinating world of a writer?

For the past seven years, I've risen early and gone to work at a coffee shop or a library. I sit in my corner and write and write and drink coffee and write some more. However, my life has shifted slightly since November of last year.

I rented out an office. After seven years, I needed another venue in which to create.

To the people who work in close proximity to my office, I am an enigma. When they ask how my weekend was, I shush them and shoo them away. When they want to tell me about their holiday plans, I shush them and shoo them away. When they mention the weather, I glare.

It's an oddity of mine, that I cannot write in solitude. I must be in a public place, surrounded by people. Open office, coffee shop, library, a plane. Even the beach works. But no one is allowed to speak to me. Especially not about the weather, Keith. Grow up.

I am pleased with the milestone, ten Mackenzie mysteries. Sometimes I wonder how long I can keep living this lovely dream. How many mysteries can Mackenzie solve? Is he near the end? Then I remember that my favorite series are between 20-50 books long. Here's hoping Mackenzie can reach such loft peaks.

Special thanks to Jan, who first brought the idea that a place like Goodwill would be ideal for stealing DNA.

Please consider leaving a review, good or bad. Your feedback online and in the wide world keeps guys like me in business.

. . .

More books on the way. Soon.

-Alan

CPSIA information can be obtained
at www.ICGtesting.com
Printed in the USA
LVHW101554250622
722116LV00004B/387

9 798811 237241